PARALYZED EMOTIONS

VIOLA TEMPEST

CONTENTS

PARALYZED EMOTIONS

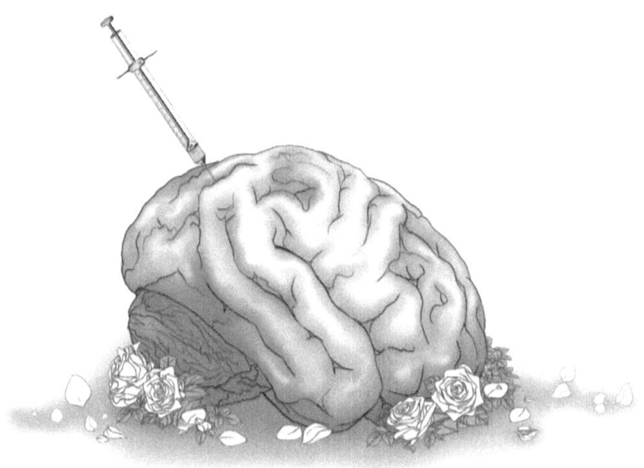

VIOLA TEMPEST

PROLOGUE

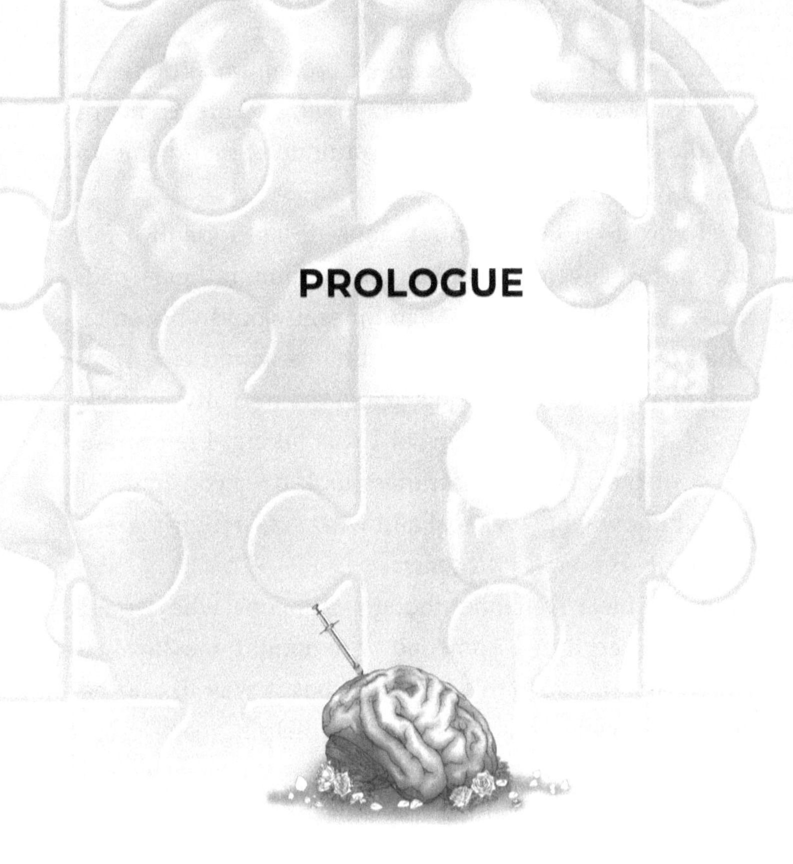

Hi, my name is Constance Fay. Two years ago, I was captured and forced into Bellevue Psychiatric Hospital against my will. But I was made to believe it had been my choice.

Here is my story.

The thing about Bellevue, is that nothing is what it seems, at least, not on the inside.

I was admitted into the hospital for one reason, but soon enough, I started doubting what that reason had been. I was fed lies and was left broken and confused. My skin was violated against my will, and the feeling of needles piercing through me continue to haunt me to this day.

I was used like a lab rat, abused, lied to, and it felt like torture, even worse than any nightmare I ever had. I used to feel so much that, at times, I wouldn't even be able to think straight, and nightmares would cloud my judgement. Pills after pills were fed into my system, and I didn't even know what I was taking. I felt afraid most of the time, and darkness took over constantly. I didn't know what was real and what was a nightmare.

Maybe it was all a nightmare.

I did meet someone, though. Someone who would change everything, someone who taught me how to laugh again, and reminded me what it was like to be alive. We spent our days together, helping each other heal and remember. Trying to figure out what was real and what was not, sifting together through our memories to try and figure out the truth. The truth about ourselves. The truths about the hospital and it's director, Dr. Theodore Faulkner.

Our torturer.

But all that is forgotten now. Thinking about it is almost like looking at a movie through a dirty glass. I can remember everything that happened. I remember the stingy pain of needles being plunged into my skin, the black ink spilling down the walls, the nightmares, the pills being shoved down my throat. I remember the last time I saw him. The last time I saw Kai. I remember blood, so much blood. But the dread is gone.

When I think about it, about every single memory of my time at the hospital and what came after, the drama that came before and led me there… I feel nothing. I'm happy.

So stupidly, irrationally happy. Everything's fine. So, I look back in my journals, endless documents of those days. On all the pain and dread. I let it all sink in; I let it get into my skin. But it doesn't. I'm happy, so I place my father's gun against my forehead while I read.

Everything's fine. Just fine. Perfectly fine.

CHAPTER
ONE

The night was dark; the crows were cawing in the far distance. A quiet whimpering disturbed the eerie silence that fell heavy on the bleak and solitary hospital room inside the adult ward of Bellevue Psychiatric Hospital. Inside, lied a young woman, me, my appearance sickly thin and pale. My frail body was curled up on a small metal bed frame, my breaths flowing heavily from my mouth.

I didn't know what was going on, or why I was so

frightened, but my mind was stuck in an empty dream, floating in a pool of black, aimlessly. It was a thick black oozing liquid that took over everything. A heavy darkness that surrounded me, pressing into my body, stealing the air out of my lungs. And inside that darkness, a pair of glowing yellow eyes watched me. Waiting, watching, piercing me.

Needles were stuck into my arms, stabbing me over and over. A knife, a small bottle of pills, a bottle of something else. A blanket, restrained in my arms, screaming. So much screaming. The beeping of machines all around me, a sterile and eerie room, the walls black with the oozing liquid, but that seemed wrong. They should be white. There should be lights shining into my eyes.

And suddenly, a casual smile tried to get to me through all the darkness, a sincere piece of happiness ripping through the blackness with teeth and nails, but the black mass took it, ate it. It took him, and I was left alone once more. Alone in the emptiness of it all.

However, it wasn't the darkness and the shadows that left me whimpering in fear for hours on end; I was used to all that. They usually went away when I wrapped the security blanket I had kept since childhood around me, keeping me safe.

No, it was what lurked beyond the darkness that kept my sweat and tears pouring, draining my essence until I became the void that lurked around me. Every emotion that I couldn't feel bombarded me, and no matter how hard I screamed, it all just wouldn't stop. I desperately wanted to be free from it all. I was willing to try anything.

I continued to toss and turn, my blanket falling over onto the cold cement floor. I then shivered from the sudden chill blowing into my room. The shiver quickly turned into violent shakes, forcing me awake. Three in the morning was never the best time for me. What was I even doing? I didn't belong here.

I tried to keep myself warm, wrapping my slender arms around my emaciated body. I sat up and felt my oversized white jacket slipping off one side of my shoulder. As I scanned the room for anything unfamiliar, my heart began to beat quicker in my chest.

However, as expected, there wasn't much to be seen. Nothing but a chair and a doorless closet, filled with the same monochrome colored clothing I had been wearing for the past several months. Hell, this cell of a room barely had a window to shine the moonlight in, only a thin sliver of glass pressed against the thick walls. And the light above me? Nothing but dimness as it flicked on once every twelve hours. Sometimes I wondered if a prison cell would've been more spacious.

My head was pounding, and my bladder felt ready to explode. Walking over to the bathroom every night proved to be a nightmare. None of the inmates, I mean patients, were allowed the privilege of their own private bathrooms, forcing us to travel down several halls just to empty ourselves out. But making that trek during the nighttime proved to be much worse than during the day. When the lights were out, the crazies came out too, turning my trip to the bathroom into a nightmare on death row.

As I stood up from my bed, my legs almost crumbled beneath the weight of my body. The room spun like crazy around me as I tried to steady myself from falling by grasping onto the metal post. Even in motion, the chill continued to pierce against me. Why won't it leave me alone? I turned toward the sliver of the window and hissed as the cold bit into my skin. I tugged at the jacket, pulling it over my shoulders again, just to watch it slip off.

God damn.

My stomach twisted and turned as I proceeded toward the wooden door. However, the pain was so unbearable, like sharp knives stabbing into my wounds. I doubled over with a groan, trying not to throw up, blood or bile, God only knew what. It felt like days since I last ate anything; not like anything was going to come up, anyway.

I picked myself up, but time after time when I tried to stand up, my stomach cramped, causing even more pain than before. I tried taking a few deep breaths again, hoping that the pain was just due to nerves.

After a few deep breaths slowly through my nostrils, and trying not to focus on the agonizing pain, I finally straightened my body up, ready to try again. I took no more than two steps before the pain forced me to hunch over yet again as I tumbled down and dragged my feet across the cold flood. It felt like I hadn't moved in months, my joints and muscles so weak I didn't even know how I was still standing.

Several agonizing moments later, I finally reached the wooden door and pressed my forehead up against it, letting out a loud groan. My body was still shivering. I couldn't understand why everything was so fucking cold. For a moment, I thought about crawling back over to the metal frame and grabbing my blanket off the ground, but I knew I didn't have the strength to make it. The added weight would just hold me in my place.

Reaching my right hand up along the door, I frantically searched along the board for a handle. No luck. Nothing but splinters and glass. After several more tries, I gave up and slid back away from the door, staring at the object with my own eyes. No wonder I couldn't find a handle; there was no handle to grab onto, nothing resembling an actual door other than the few hinges along the side of the frame. I remembered a handle; why wasn't it there?

"Hello?" I called out hesitantly, hitting my hand against the door with every ounce of energy I could muster up.

The sound of my palm slapping against the metal echoed through the room, and an unbearable ringing started in my ears. I squeezed my eyes shut, focusing on anything but the pain, and continued knocking with the little strength I had left.

Then I saw it, a shadow, the creepy shadow in my dreams. I shifted my body back in tension and fear. I heard scraping against the other side of the door, a panel sliding over to the left before bright yellow eyes came into my vision. My eyes burned from the intensity of the creature's eyes, and I flinched back even more, stumbling over the jacket that had completely fallen off my shoulders.

"Hello?" I asked again but with little confidence.

Despite the haunting shadow, at least that confirmed that I wasn't alone, I wasn't sure if this bright-eyed creature was any better than solitude, but maybe my imagination was just running amuck. Either way, I had to find out what was going on. I didn't belong here, yet, here I was, with no answers or hint of a way out.

"Hello? Can you help me? Why am I here?" I called out once again, expecting another response of silence, when I heard a deep voice call out.

"Back up, darling," the voice of a man called out, his voice squeezing into the room through the small constructed window.

I frowned, ignoring his warning and only stepped closer to the door. I could hear chiseling and scraping on the other side, and was curious as to what was going on. I reached over to the spot where the sound was coming from, just to quickly pull my hand back into my stomach and wince.

"What the hell? You scraped me!" I shouted in pain as red marks formed along my fingertips. "Tell me what's going on, right now!"

"I warned you to back up," his voice was deeper this time, and sounded like he was trying not to laugh.

"I want answers," I responded.

It was a wonder to me why I was trying to be defiant. It probably would have been easier to get answers if I listened to him, but my head was too heavy to even attempt to think straight.

He let out an annoyed sigh and then disappeared.

Confused, I pressed my forehead against the door and tried to look out past the window into the hallway, but all I could see was a door right across from mine and the walls on either side of it.

"Please!" I called out into the hall.

I jerked my head back and nearly stumbled to the ground. The sudden movement caused my stomach to cramp again, but it didn't hold a candle to the fear that shook the rest of my body. A stick with a metal-pointed end was sticking through the slot, and the bright-eyed man wielding it laughed again. I held up my hands and lowered my head as a sign of obedience.

He was a monster, laughing like a maniac with his twisted teeth and scary eyes. He was a nightmare that came to reality to haunt me.

A second later, as if on a timer, the door unlocked and slid open. I watched as two white shoes came into my line of vision, and I slowly traveled up the length of the man's body and settled on his face, successfully taking him all in.

His eyes weren't as bright as I thought they were, and his shadow was nothing out of the ordinary like the one in my nightmares. He wasn't very tall, and his face looked pinched. Like his mother squished his cheeks together too much as a child, and it stayed like that for the rest of his life.

He was still holding the stick, jabbing the pointed end into his own hand to look menacing. Or maybe he was just holding it. It would have worked if he weren't wearing rainbow scrubs. Finally, he let out a sigh and dropped the stick to his side, tapping the tip of it against the ground.

"Good morning, Ms. Fay," he said in a falsely sweet smile as he took a large step toward my direction, the sound of his step trembling against the Earth.

I stepped back, wanting to keep a good distance between us. Given the dimensions of the room though, I figured that would be nearly impossible to do. My eyes darted to the stick he still held in his hand and wondered what he would have done if I continued to rebel.

"Ms. Fay, do you know where you are?" he asked, looking around the room. Disappointment crossed his face when he noticed that the blanket was on the ground. "Tsk, you know that you have to keep this room clean. It is not yours."

I was about to tell him off, order him to give me some answers, and let me out of here, but all that came out was, "What do you mean this isn't my room?"

He gave me a tired look before bending down to pick the blanket off the ground. I almost lost it when he brought it up to his nose and sniffed it before placing it back down onto the bed.

"You're just a guest here," he spoke with such sincerity. "You wouldn't stay at a friend's house and just leave all your belongings scattered across their floor, now, would you?"

Suddenly, I saw it again. The bright glow deep inside his eyes sprouted up once again, a glow so bright that it blinded me, a sharp pain zipping across my head as I stumbled back and scraped my skeletal knees against the sharp frame of the bed.

The man rushed forward, grabbing hold of my shoulders and steadying me. "Are you okay?" he asked.

My body froze. His hands felt so cold, like a block of ice, and up close, his eyes looked even more menacing. I struggled to look him in the eyes. My body was shaking faster than ever, but I didn't want to risk making a move that would potentially get me killed.

My heart pounded faster as I saw him reach inside his body, my instincts telling me a knife was on the other side. If he was willing to stab me before, what's to stop him from doing it again?

"Whoa, whoa! What are you doing? What is that? Are you trying to kill me?" I shouted as I tried to twist my body away from him, stopping when I heard the sound of a simple click.

A simple flashlight.

"Calm down, Ms. Fay. It's just a flashlight. I just need to make sure your vitals are stable."

For someone who was just accused of attempted murder, he sounded awfully calm. He grabbed the back of my head to keep me from jerking as he flashed the blinding light straight into my eye.

"Nothing too out of the ordinary," he said as he clicked the light off. "How are you feeling today?" He checked my pulse with two fingers against my wrist while he waited for an answer.

So much had happened in such a short period of time that I couldn't tell the difference between my fear and my confusion. I climbed up and slumped my limp body back against the wall and closed my eyes. Everything was piling up in my head so quickly that I couldn't focus on what to say next. It was beginning to be too much, and all I wanted to do was lie in bed underneath the blanket until it sorted itself out again.

"Ms. Fay. Ms. Fay, wake up! You're dozing off again," I heard a voice whisper deep inside my head again as my body was jostled.

I opened up my eyes slowly and saw the bright-yellow eyes once again, my pale skin turning a shade of green in response. I covered my mouth and breathed through my nose quickly to dispel the feeling of vomiting right then and there.

"Stop, please stop," I begged against my hand.

I looked up at him, and he quickly withdrew his hand from my shoulder. "I'm feeling sick to my stomach," I muttered, letting my hand fall onto my lap. I stared down at the lines on my palm for a moment before looking up again. "Why am I here? Where am I?"

He clasped his hands behind his back, his voice suddenly soft. "You are at Bellevue Psychiatric Hospital. You were brought in a few months ago after you threatened to set your parents' house on fire with them and yourself in it, well, according to your file, anyway. I've only just been assigned to your care. Your family didn't feel safe with you around, so they sent you here. You don't remember?"

I frowned in disbelief. That didn't make much sense. Why would I be at my parents' house? I was twenty-seven. Was I staying over? The last time I had been with my parents was for Christmas. Was it around Christmas?

"That doesn't make any sense," I told him. "Why can't I remember that?"

"It was a traumatic event for everyone involved, and your brain must have blocked it out from your working memory," he told me. "It happens all the time with patients who experience trauma." He checked my eyes again before standing straight. "Stay here. I'll be right back."

Before I could get another word out, the door was locked again, and the strange man was gone. I blinked a few times and shivered again. I grabbed the blanket that was now balled up on my bed and wrapped it around my shoulders.

Left alone in my room, my head started spinning, and I thought I could hear voices whispering to me.

"Bellevue is a dark, dangerous place," they told me.

"You should get out of here; you'll never be the same ever again."

I pressed my hands against my ears, trying to shush the voices in my head. I didn't know much about Bellevue Hospital, but I vaguely remembered the stories. I remembered people whispering about this place, about weird experiments being done in the dark basement, about people leaving not the same way they entered.

But how could I know what was real and what was not? Had I really heard any of that, or was it just my mind conjuring up stories because I was scared? More than scared, I was terrified. I couldn't remember where

I'd been the last three months of my life, if what the mysterious man with yellow glowing eyes had said was right.

In that precise moment, I could barely remember the night before, or even the dream I just had a few minutes prior. So, how could I know if anything my mind was whispering to me was even real?

"You know what's real; you just need to push past the fog," a male voice whispered inside my head.

No, no, no. I couldn't do that. There was too much pain behind that curtain of fog; that fog was what was keeping me sane. But, was I even sane? I wanted to scream out loud; the burning in my lungs was getting unbearable.

What was real? What was not? I wanted out. I needed to get out of this horrible cell. The walls were pressing in on me, and the voices wouldn't shut up.

Just as my eyes were getting too heavy to keep open, as the walls were finally closing in on me, killing me, the door unlocked again. I lifted my head and watched as the same man came in with a glass of water and some pills. I looked down at the small white pills and gulped. I had never been a fan of taking medication. It felt wrong going down my throat no matter how I took them.

"I don't want them," I told him quietly.

"I'm not asking. I'm telling," he told me. "Take the pills. They'll help with the headaches and the nausea. Swallow them, and I'll take you out to the yard."

"The yard?" I asked innocently.

The pills rattled inside the cup as he shook his head. "With the other patients. Non-violent, of course."

"I don't want to—"

"You have to. Take the pills so we can get going." He sighed.

It was clear that he had enough of me already.

"I'm not taking them! I'm not taking anything you're giving me! You're trying to kill me!" I yelled all of a sudden, all the fear and anger I was feeling exploding out of me as I knocked the cup out of his hand.

"Ms. Fay, that was very rude," the man said in a calm tone, almost too calm. He moved over to the floor and picked up the pills, his eyes never leaving me. "Please, take them. Trust me, you'll love the yard. You haven't been out there in a long time; the sun and fresh air will be good for you."

I cowered back against the wall, looking at him with huge scared eyes. "You're not lying to me? I can really go outside?" I asked in a small, shattered voice.

"You have my word," he said solemnly.

I swallowed hard and snagged the pills he had picked up, and the water as well, as he stretched his hands out closer to my face. The pills rolled around the bottom of the cup, and I let out a shaky breath. I closed my eyes before tossing the pills into my mouth and chasing them down with the entire cup of water.

The pills forced their way down my throat, scrapping the inside of my throat on their way in, and I focused on the man's chest. The feeling made me gag, and I had to do everything in my power not to send them back up. It was causing tears to form in my eyes.

The man sighed and popped his hip out to the side.

"I hate when you're dramatic," he mumbled almost too low for me to hear, snatching the small cup away from me.

Did he really say that? Or was it all inside my mind? He waited until the pained expression left my face before helping me to my feet.

"Alright, come on."

My body was still shaking as I leaned more into him than I would have liked to, but I didn't care. I couldn't care. It slowly got easier to walk though as the medication started to take effect.

As we approached the gates, I could hear loud screams and what sounded like a trashy reality show. I glanced up at the man.

"Do I have to?" I asked, not sure how I was going to like this.

I felt anxious and uneasy about seeing people; I felt like I'd been alone for so long.

He gave me a smug look before helping me stand straight again and opening the door.

"You don't have a choice, Princess. Go out. You'll like it."

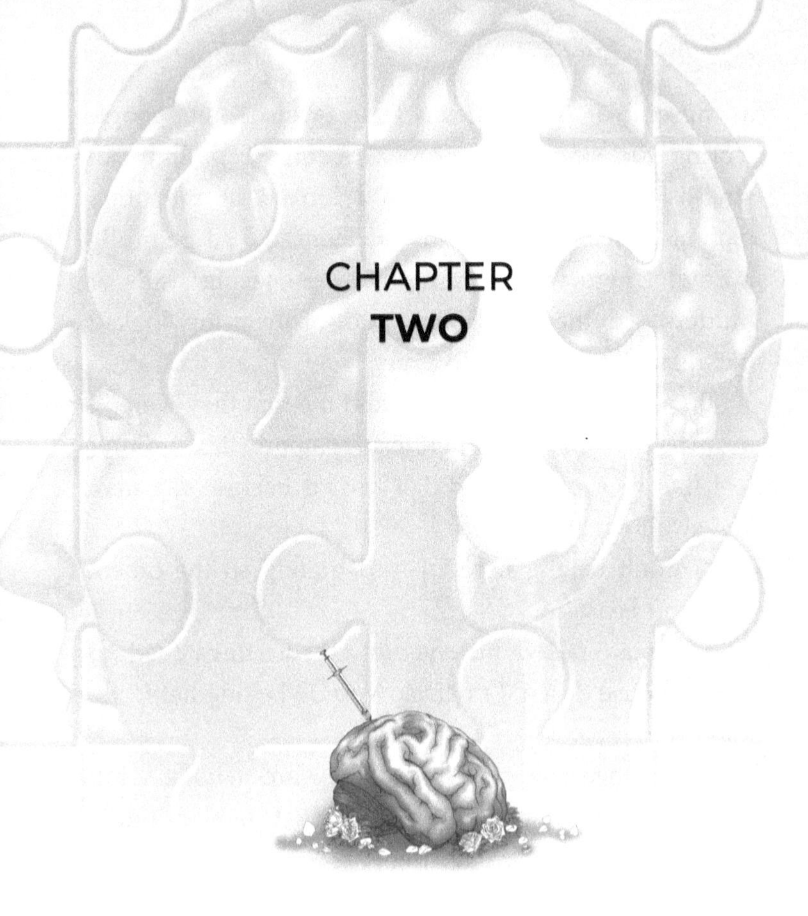

CHAPTER
TWO

I looked around the yard when I stepped out, and I scrunched up my nose as I was assaulted by the smell of at least fifty people crammed into one tiny gated yard. At least, it wasn't as cold as my room was. The sun was warm against my skin, and that was a relief. It felt like a blessing to have the warmth tickling my skin, and I closed my eyes against the brightness for a second, taking in the pleasant sensation.

Everyone crammed in that weeded yard looked just

as miserable as the next. There were some people tearing the skin off their bodies, others pulling out strands of hair. However, as I looked at the other patients, I realized that most of them looked painfully normal. There were a few who were facing walls or muttering to themselves, but a lot of them just looked like regular people, just like me.

But something in my head told me that they weren't normal. I wasn't normal either apparently, but I didn't feel like they probably did. I turned back to the man and swallowed hard.

"I don't belong here," I said quietly so the others wouldn't hear.

The man raised his eyebrow. "You threatened to burn a house down. I'm afraid you do belong here," he told me.

He pushed me gently into the yard with a wink before walking away and locking the gate behind him.

I stumbled forward, feeling eyes turn to look at me. I closed my eyes and took a deep breath to calm myself down. It was probably just my paranoia. As soon as they caught a quick glimpse of me, everyone who had first turned looked away. It still felt like everyone was staring at me though, and it made my stomach twist.

It took a few seconds for me to regain my composure, and I started to walk toward the chair that was pressed against the far wall that faced the outside world I so much struggled to remember, a world I couldn't remember ever living in.

My memory was getting the best of me. I couldn't remember being stuck in this hospital for more than a couple months, so why couldn't I remember life anywhere else but here? I could picture the faces of my family, my parents, and a few facts about my life, but I couldn't remember the exact moment I was admitted into the hospital, or why, how I had gotten here.

I settled into the chair as I saw other patients do the same, all wishing they didn't belong here. I looked over to my left and saw a pair arguing, most of the sounds high-pitched and animated. Sometimes I wondered, was I crazy before coming here, or did all of this drive me there, a constructed stage to bring seemingly normal people together just to brand them as insane?

I did remember something that seemed to be from when I first got here, maybe the first few weeks. A burly woman, or at least I hoped was a woman, had tried to start a fight with me to assert her dominance. But I wasn't about that life, that drama. I didn't come here to get pushed around like a prisoner. I'd respond much better to those who were civilized and treated me like a decent human being.

Then again, the yellow-eyed man did tell me that I had threatened to burn down my parents' home. I didn't think I was even capable of something like that, but apparently, I was. Did I actually start the fire, though? Would that make me a violent patient, a criminal, instead of someone who acted impulsively and lost control in that very moment?

The questions clouding my brain were starting to hurt my head again, so I turned my focus to the people around me, instead. There were honestly too many of them for the size of this dinky yard we were in. It was barely larger than the size of the cold room I had been sleeping in.

It became hard to keep track of who was who too, but some of their faces were vaguely familiar. There was a woman who looked oddly similar to me, dressed in the same oversized white jacket that I was wearing. The bottom was torn and frayed like mine from when I kept picking the exposed threads out and putting them in a pile.

There was also a guy to my right who kept watching and imitating a nurse. The nurse wasn't doing anything, except maybe talking with the other nurses. She had a silly smile plastered on her face, completely ignorant of the weird people doing weird things in front of her. She seemed so immune to it all, but maybe that's how it was after a sane person was exposed to the crazy for such a long time.

The guy would watch the nurse and then use a crayon to write something down as quickly as he could. Whenever the nurse looked over, he'd put the piece of paper under his leg and look away like he wasn't doing anything. The nurse would always give a knowing smile before shaking her head and going back to her conversation with the other nurses.

It was so odd.

There was an older man in the farthest corner from me. He was sitting at a tiny table with two chairs, in front of a chess board. He'd think for a while, move one of the white pieces, and then he'd jump chairs, going to the other side of the table and thinking for a long time before moving a black piece. He kept repeating the same pattern, thinking, moving, and then changing from one side of the board to the other. He'd run his fingers through his ashen hair every once in a while, and then bite his lip. His lips would then move slowly, as if he was talking to himself, and the sight made me so nervous I had to look the other way.

A few feet away from me, there was a girl sitting on the floor. She couldn't be more than eighteen years old. There were no kids in this hospital, so that's why I knew her age, but in all honesty, she was so frail and small that she seemed to be barely fourteen. She had a stack of dry leaves from the trees as well as little sticks, and she spread them out all over the floor. They were classified by shape, color, and size, a perfect arrangement of dead nature. It was oddly satisfying to watch her measure the leaves against each other, over and over again.

I kept looking around, trying to find little details about the people around me. There was one guy that seemed completely out of it. He was talking to himself, settling down closest to the outside world. He was sitting on the grass, his legs folded over each other, with his feet resting over his knees.

I tried to strain my hearing to see if I could pick up on his words, but the arguing couple next to me was getting louder and louder. I kept watching him though, trying to figure out what he was on about. It took me a while, but I finally realized he wasn't talking to himself, but rather talking to the tree on the other side of the fence. He was gesturing with his hands as he was telling it a story, or that's what I thought.

I sighed, happy that I wasn't like any of them. If I were, then I would rather not be seen by anyone. I would be happy living away in the little room they had me trapped in. It would be less embarrassing that way.

"People watching, huh?" a handsome man asked as he fell into the spot next to me.

I jumped and looked over at him. I wasn't used to feeling so jumpy, and I wasn't sure if my heart could take another scare, especially not after the events from the morning. I looked at the man before me for a moment before turning my head away from his radiant smile.

"I'm not here to talk."

The man frowned and shifted on his seat. He looked out to everyone around us. The frown didn't last long, and he was smiling again.

"Oh, come on. You have to talk to me. I'm the most interesting person here," he teased. He nudged me and quickly leaned back at the disgusted look on my face. "I'm only playing. I'm probably the most boring person you'll ever meet."

"Then why are you even talking to me?" I sighed, wiping a hand across my arm where he'd touched me.

He clearly didn't get the hint.

He shrugged innocently and held out a hand. "I'm Kai Hastings."

I stared at his hand before looking up at him. I gave him a loose handshake before pulling my hand back into my lap.

"Constance Fay."

"I know," he said with a wide grin.

My frown matched the size of his grin. "What do you mean? How do you know?" I asked.

I didn't like someone new just knowing who I was. It was different when it was a nurse, a doctor, or the creepy man with bright yellow eyes who seemed to know so much about my existence here. He probably had seen my file a million times in the few months that I had been here.

But this was a man I just met. I couldn't remember ever seeing him in the hallways before, not like I had many memories of them, anyway. He was someone who shouldn't know anything about me. As far as I knew, the only place I'd spent time in since I got here was in my room.

There was no way that he could know me. Was there? Had I been in this yard before? Why couldn't I remember that? I felt like I had been in this same chair before, like I was having some sort of déjà vu.

Kai shrugged his shoulders and leaned back against the chair beside me. He pushed himself up before falling onto his foot after he tucked it underneath himself.

"I just know things," he told me. He tapped a finger against his temple as he winked. "It's a superpower of mine."

"Oh, great, another crazy one," I murmured.

I turned away and caught sight of a woman trying to flirt with a nurse to get a double dosing of her daily meds.

"I've got a secret for you," Kai told me despite my blatant attempts at ignoring him.

He poked my arm when I didn't look over. His finger pressed almost directly against the bone, and the smile disappeared quickly from his face.

When I turned, he quickly turned it back to his megawatt smile. He didn't want me to see him concerned or upset. It wasn't the right time.

"Stop touching me," I growled, pushing his finger away.

"But I've got a secret," he insisted.

"I don't care."

"Yes, you do."

"No, I don't."

"I know that you do. Do you want to know why?"

I groaned and pulled my knees to my chest to hide my face away.

"Please, leave me alone," I practically begged.

A nurse walked over to us with a frown on her face.

"Is everything alright over here?" she asked, looking between the two of us.

"Yes," Kai said before words could exit my mouth. "We're just talking. You know how it is. Sometimes people bicker. Don't worry about it."

I opened my mouth to speak, but the words fell back down my throat as the nurse started walking away. I turned slowly to face Kai.

"We're not bickering. I want you to go away, and you're refusing to leave."

"I only want to talk, Constance," he told me. He softened his smile and lowered his head a little to look more welcoming. "I promise… that's all I want to do."

I let out a heavy sigh before turning to fully face him.

"Fine." I gave in.

"Fine?" he asked, his smile widening again.

"Yes! But I don't want to hear about any secrets you have. I don't need some crazy guy whispering conspiracy theories in my ear."

I'd overheard one of the crazies arguing about the government hiding the fact that there were lizard people living among us and posing as politicians to take over the Earth. I didn't need any further craziness like that.

"That's fine with me," he told me. He wiggled a bit as he got more comfortable in his seat. He looked around the room, biting his lip before nodding. "Okay, who do you think has been here the longest?"

"I think I'm going to have to go with the man talking to the tree," I responded, giving in as I knew he wasn't going down without a fight.

Surprisingly, we continued talking for the rest of the day. I didn't want to admit that I enjoyed his company, but I did. He seemed more normal than the people surrounding us, though, some of them didn't seem to be too far gone, which was good.

I was simply happy to have someone to talk to, even if for a little bit. As I curled up in my stiff, cold bed that night, I figured I could survive my short stay here.

At least, I hoped it was short.

CHAPTER
THREE

The next morning, I found myself in the same spot as the day before. I was one of the first ones in the yard and couldn't be less thrilled. Despite the length of time, it was difficult to see how people could remain so occupied with absolutely nothing to do other than pick at our own fingernails. It also felt a lot smaller than the day before. With all these people, I found it easier to toss and turn in my own bed.

I struggled to relax and remain in my own thoughts

with so many people trying to have conversations around me all at once, screaming at each other. I wanted so desperately to ask one of the nurses to let me go back inside to spare my mind from this trash around me. But after getting rejected and ignored so many times, it just seemed like wasted breath to try again at this point.

I was chewing on my nail as I continued to stare at the bickering couple before me. My eyes were glued to the woman on the left like a screw, the one who I thought resembled me. She was a very odd-looking woman, her hair tied in six different hairstyles, and her clothing torn only on one side. When she saw me staring, she came over to me and stood a few inches away, looking down at me.

"You look like I used to when I was younger," she said, and then started to chew on her nail.

I looked up at her, and then looked back down. I didn't want to talk to her; I wasn't in the mood to make any friends here, and God damn, if I find out I have a relative here.

"What's your name?" she asked me. "I'm Cadence; you can call me Cady if you want. I don't remember if we've met before."

"Constance," I said in a low voice, feeling too rude not to reply to a direct question. "And you can call me Connie if you like it better."

"Great. We are friends now."

With that, Cadence walked away and stood by the outside fence, her eyes lost in the distance as she seemed to stare into nothing. She seemed smarter than the rest of the patients somehow, like she was hiding something that no one else knew about.

Kai walked into the yard not too long after that and spotted me. He grinned and bounced over to me before falling into the seat next to mine. He laughed as I bounced slightly from the startle that he gave me. I almost felt like I was having a heart attack, if the pills I had been forcibly taking didn't already push down any emotions I had left inside my body. He propped his elbow up on the back of his chair and turned his eyes to the same couple before me.

"You know," he started, successfully scaring me out of the trance the quarrel had on me. "My aunt used to behave like this all the time, always bickering and never accepting defeat, even though she knew she no longer had any ground to stand on."

I held a hand to my chest with my eyes shut as I took in steady breaths. My eyes opened only when he stopped talking, and he turned to look at me.

"You have got to stop scaring me," I told him.

I didn't want to be related to anyone in here… except maybe Kai.

"Sorry, it's a problem of mine. I'm just too quiet. I always snuck up on my parents as a kid without trying, and my older brother told me it's what gave my dad the heart attack that killed him," he told me.

I held a hand up between us and shook my head. "I just got so much information about your family in such a short amount of time. I think we need to talk about both incidents separately, and then I should be able to digest it."

Kai laughed quietly and nodded. "Alright, alright," he told me, trying not to laugh more. "My Aunt Shelby was my dad's older sister. She was an adorable little lady, but she was also crazy, old, and cranky. She was that typical lady in the neighborhood who knew everything that was going on with everybody else, even if she had no business in any of them. She loved the gossip as much as she loved her bickering. It didn't really matter what she believed in; she'd always go against whatever point we were trying to make. If I said salads were healthy, she'd find something against them and tell me I couldn't only live on salad if that was all I ever ate. Eventually, I'd give in and end up seeing that they weren't really that healthy, right?" Kai kept talking and talking, his eyes never leaving me as he told me story after story about her aunt's silly arguments against everything and everybody.

He moved onto talking about his father after that, telling me about how he'd died of a heart attack all of a sudden. It had taken a really hard toll on his family, and his mother had to struggle to keep the family afloat while working two part-time jobs at the same time. He talked about her with longing admiration, and I could tell that, despite their differences, they'd had a great and loving relationship.

———

As the day went on, I found myself hanging onto every story Kai had told. He had a lot of them, too. It was like I was living inside a story book. It made the day go by much faster, and I barely noticed if we had already had our morning pills and lunch or not. All the hours of the day seemed to fuse together, and I lost track of it, not really knowing which part of the day I was stuck in.

When we were settled on the chairs again, probably after lunch, I decided to take on the story telling. There was something that had been bothering me since I woke up the day before.

"I don't feel right being here," I told him quietly. I glanced at him before sitting up straighter. "Not in a 'I'm not crazy' kind of way, but more with the fact that this place just seems off."

"It *is* a mental hospital, after all; it tends to give the off vibe," he reminded me. He turned and crossed his legs on the chair. He rested his elbows on his knees, and then his chin on his hands. "But please, tell me more."

"Well… after I showered this morning, I saw something on my stomach that doesn't fit in with any part of my life or what I remember or what was told to me," I whispered. After making sure that no one was looking at us, I raised my shirt and showed him the scar that crossed over my stomach. "A few days ago, I didn't have this scar. I was clean. Fine. But after… after… seeing the man with the bright yellow eyes, this scar just started to mysteriously appear out of thin air."

Kai looked at the scar, and then looked up at me. It looked like he wanted to touch it, but he respectfully kept his eager hands to himself.

"The man with bright yellow eyes? Is he a patient here? I don't remember seeing him around, and I know a lot of people here," he said, tilting his head to the side.

"Yes! He came into my room a few days ago, told me he was a nurse, and that I threatened to burn down my parents' house with everyone still in it," I whispered. My eyes got wide, and I sat up quickly, putting my hands up. "I didn't though. At least, I don't think I did. It couldn't have been me. I couldn't honestly ever hurt my parents or commit such a crime. I just... I can't remember anything else."

Kai frowned and glanced around quickly. "Can I tell you my secret now?" he asked, moving closer to me. "I promise that it might help shine some light on the dark parts of your memory."

I groaned and shook my head. "No, I don't want to hear your secret," I mumbled.

It was easy to forget where we were when we were just talking about normal family things. I didn't want to be reminded about why we were both here. I didn't want to know why Kai was here. I was happy to wait in blissful ignorance until I was allowed out. If he started acting crazy, then I would have to wait out the rest of my days in the hospital alone.

Kai let his shoulders sag, and he nodded.

"Okay, fine," he whispered softly. "I won't say it, yet. But I want you to remember that I know something you might need to know."

I sighed but nodded.

"I'll keep that in mind," I told him. "I think I might try to take a nap. The food might be the worst, but it makes me tired." I shifted on the chair and let my head fall back before closing my eyes.

Kai laughed quietly and looked around us.

"Good luck," he told me. "I doubt you'll be able to sleep here."

"I can sleep anywhere," I assured him. "Just make sure none of the weirdos come near me."

"I will be your ever-faithful knight," he told me with a smile.

He rested his head on his hand as he propped his elbow against the back of the chair.

He watched as my breathing evened out, and my clenched hands loosened enough to show that I was finally relaxed. It must hurt to see me as lost as I was, and all he could do was hope that I would listen to him one day.

CHAPTER
FOUR

I had spent the week after that with that mindset. I didn't bring up feelings in the conversations with Kai again. I didn't want to ruin the experience I was having. I could barely remember the last time I had an actual good time.

Before my dark days, or the days I couldn't remember at all, I remembered spending Christmas at home. It was one of the last memories I had from everything that had happened before the hospital. One of the few that had come back to me only just recently. I just finished my semester at grad school and was ready to take the much-needed time off. I had been struggling a bit at school; my grades weren't as good as they used to be for some reason, but I couldn't remember exactly why.

I had fun then. It wasn't anything much, though. Just opening a few presents, having a few drinks, and spending time with family I rarely ever saw. But then I'd left and went back to my apartment, the one I shared with my best friend. I didn't really want to think about it, but for some reason, the memory kept poking at my brain.

I had walked into the apartment, all the holiday joy still lingering inside of me, and I opened the door to find… to find my best friend on the couch with my boyfriend, Kyle. I remembered my utter disbelief as I looked at them curled up together, so confident with one another. Leg over leg, and arms tangled in hair. A mass of limbs interlocked together. I think I yelled. Maybe I yelled.

Or I cried. I'm not really sure.

It took him a long time to get me to calm down, and after a few days of coming and going, of begging and apologizing, of presents and flowers and chocolate and so many 'It was a mistake,' I caved in. We ended up back together, pretending, or trying to pretend, that nothing had happened.

My friend moved out. My boyfriend moved in.

It was what was meant to happen, or that's what I told myself. I had spoken with one of my other friends about it, and she had insisted I was stupid for going back to him. But we've been together for almost five years, and I wasn't going to throw all that away over one silly mistake. I wasn't willing to forget about every single good moment we've had together because he had cheated on me once.

Or I hoped it was only once. I never talked to my roommate again; I didn't want to hear her excuses. She had tried to blame it all on my boyfriend, and that wasn't fair.

Kyle and I talked about it, set our differences aside, and he explained to me why he had felt so distant from me lately. He'd said I was changing, but that he still loved me and wanted to stay with me. That he wanted us to work it all out. So, we did. He apologized over and over, we made peace, and we moved on... It was what was best for all of us.

All the fun I had while away was balled up and tossed into the back of my mind after I entered the apartment. Hidden away from me like all the rest. And the pain from the realization was blurry. It was how I knew how to function. It made me feel safe. All the happy memories were protected from my own self-deprecating mind.

But when I was there, talking with Kai about his life and hearing all his wild stories, I was happy. Well, almost happy. It was the closest I was going to get. I didn't think that I would ever be genuinely happy ever again.

As I was lying on the grass and listening to him speak, I couldn't help but imagine pictures that went along with the stories. I hadn't even realized that he stopped talking, and that I was just making up the rest of it in my head. It wasn't until he touched my arm that I did. I opened my eyes and looked at him.

"What? Is it time for therapy?" I asked.

He laughed at me and shook his head, "such a daydreamer, you are."

There were two types of therapy that every patient was expected to go to during their stay at Bellevue. Group therapy was every Tuesday and Thursday. On Mondays, Wednesdays, and Fridays, it was individual therapy.

It was a tedious and monotonous routine. Almost every day was the same, and if it wasn't for those specific activities we had once in a while, life could have just blended into one long day. The light turned on in the morning, and someone came over to make sure I was up. I'd be escorted to the bathroom, where I would use the facilities, get a shower if it was a Monday, Wednesday, or Friday, and then be escorted outside to the yard for an hour or two. Time wasn't something I was completely aware of inside that place.

After the time was up, we'd go back inside for our morning pills, or sometimes, they'd bring them over to us. Most of us were stubborn like that. We spent almost all morning out in the yard until it was time to head back inside to have the bland and boring lunch.

Lunch consisted mostly of purees and other shapeless meals that had absolutely no flavor to them. They changed color, but they all seemed to be the same crap.

If I ate it all, I'd be allowed pudding, a measly four ounces.

The afternoons blended in between therapy sessions and group activities when we sometimes got to play silly games or even watch TV all together, and then dinner would be served back in our rooms, with more pills to make sure we slept through the night.

Little did those pills do to help me with the night-mares that haunted me every time I closed my eyes, though. Those yellow bright eyes kept coming at me night after night, together with images of needles piercing my skin, knives hanging from invisible hooks on the walls, and pills rolling down my tongue.

Therapy wasn't my favorite time of the day.

I had only gone to the group therapy sessions lately, and I didn't even dare to speak there. It would mean admitting defeat, which I wasn't ready for. I didn't need to be there, which meant I didn't need to participate in their group activities.

Well, except taking pills three times a day, which I couldn't avoid. I asked what mine were for, and I was told to ask my therapist. My therapist was the one who was supposed to be having one-on-one therapy sessions with me. But for reasons I couldn't fully understand, my sessions had stopped a few weeks ago. Or had it been months?

Apparently, I hadn't been cooperating, and after I attacked my therapist by throwing something at him, they'd decided to have me in reclusion for a while. Was that why I had been locked in my room for so long? I didn't seem to be able to get a grasp on my own thoughts. It was like having a lot of information mixed up together inside my brain.

There were things I knew, but there were so many more I wasn't sure were right. I knew all this. I knew I had been in my room for weeks, knew I had been in the hospital for at least three months, but I couldn't be sure if any of that was really true.

Nothing was certain anymore. I couldn't trust my brain, and I couldn't trust what anybody was telling me, either.

And going back to the pills I was taking, I didn't believe that any doctor had actually prescribed me the medicine. I think the nurses were shoving generic pills down my throat, even if they didn't know what they were for. The thought of hiding them under my tongue had crossed my mind, but I convinced myself that someone would find out soon enough, and I would get in trouble. The image of the nurse with the stick had caused me enough worry about the kind of things they did to patients who stepped out of line, that I didn't want to experience it myself.

I blinked a few times as I realized that Kai was still speaking to me, but I had spaced out and heard none of it. I shook my head and pulled my hair out of my face.

"I'm sorry. I didn't catch a single word you said," I admitted.

Kai took a deep breath before letting it out slowly.

"I need you to really concentrate on what I'm telling you," he said each word as slowly and clearly as he could and nodded his head.

I looked him in the eyes and nodded my head along with him.

"I'm listening," I told him just as slowly.

"That nurse that you saw when you first woke up was lying," he told me quietly. He grabbed me by the shoulders and squeezed them, hoping that it would keep my attention on him. "You've been here for almost a year. When you first got here, you were sent off, your memory erased. I can't keep this secret from you any longer."

I stared at him for a long while before letting out a hysterical laugh and shaking my head. "God. I can't take you seriously," I told him. "You always have these wild stories that you tell. I don't know if half of them are even true."

"Everything I have ever told you is the truth," he said seriously. "You can always rely on that. I wouldn't lie about something like this, anyway. They're trying to feed a fake memory into your head so you'll become more compliant. You can't let them do that. Do you understand?"

I rolled my eyes and shrugged his hands off. "Give it a rest," I murmured.

"I know you don't really remember what happened, but you need to try. They came to your room. At least two or three nurses. They dragged you out of the room, and you fought against them. I heard you actually knocked one of them in the jaw before they could restrain you. They took you to one of the labs in the basement. A dingy room with no windows. One that smells stale and feels like you're inside a prison, even more than your room. They injected something in your arm and kept you under observation for days. But something went wrong. It messed with your head, and your memories got all jumbled because of it." Kai was talking while looking at me intently, and I could see images popping in my head as he did.

I pictured three large male nurses coming into my room. My fist collided against one of the guy's jaws. The nurse with the bright yellow eyes grabbed me hard from the shoulders. A dimly lit room with no windows that smelled like a doctor's office and hadn't been inhabited for months. A syringe poking into my arm. No, that was a memory from my dreams. Needles piercing my skin over and over while surrounded by darkness. It was not real; it was all a dream. A nightmare.

"None of that is real," I said weakly.

Kai groaned and dug his fingernails into his palms. "Why don't you believe me?"

"I can't believe anyone who's in the loony bin," I admitted.

I dropped my feet onto the floor and leaned my head back.

"Especially the people who work here, the doctors, the nurses," Kai replied, his tone still serious. "They're the most delusional ones out of all of us. They think they're better than us just because they don't suffer from any kind of mental illness or are better at hiding it. They think they hold power over us."

"Do you hear yourself right now?" I asked, rolling my head to the side to look at him. His face was red, and his eyes were starting to shift around as if they couldn't settle on one thing. "Why are you here?" I asked.

Kai sat back, and his eyebrows shot up.

"What?" he asked.

"You heard me. Why are you here? What did you do to get sent here?" I asked again, leaning more toward him. I tilted my head to the side.

"Why does that matter?" He frowned and looked away.

I found out later that it wasn't that he was ashamed, but that he didn't want to tell me as it would've caused me to dismiss him even more.

I smirked. "You're one of the crazy ones, aren't you? The real crazy ones. Do you hear voices in your head? Are they telling you that the nurses are out to get us?"

Kai squeezed his eyes shut. "Stop," he told me in a whisper.

If he kept his eyes shut long enough, his mind would start closing off everything else before he got too worked up.

"I'm only asking you a question, Kai." I laughed. I moved closer. "Why won't you answer it? You tell me everything about your life. Why not this?" I felt like I was the one sounding crazy now.

"I don't want you to think I'm lying," he admitted.

It was clear that he had been in this type of situation plenty of times before.

I shrugged my shoulders. "I'm going to think that, anyway. Might as well tell me the whole truth."

He put his hands in his hair and tugged on the short strands. It helped only a little to keep him focused.

"I have PTSD," he finally told me. "I take medication, and it keeps my head clear of everything. I'm only here because… I lashed out once. It was the wrong place, wrong time. But I take my meds now, so you can believe everything I say. My head is clear. As clear as it's ever been."

I stared at him. I looked over his face quickly before going to his hands in his hair as they tugged.

"I don't," I told him. "How can I believe you?"

Kai stopped suddenly and let his hands drop to his sides. Then he remembered something.

"I knew your name," he told me.

"What?" I frowned.

"I knew your name. When I first came over to talk to you, I knew your name, and you asked me how I knew it. I lied to you then, but that was only because you honestly didn't know who I was. We've spoken before," he told me quickly. "In fact, I was one of the first ones you spoke to when you first got admitted. You sat in that same spot and people-watched before you walked over to talk to me. You told me that you wanted to go home, but you knew that it was best for you to be here until you were better."

I was quiet for a while. It was hard to believe anything he said anymore.

"I still can't believe a word you say," I admitted, taking my hands to the side of my head, trying to get the voices to quiet down.

I was so confused; I didn't know what to think anymore.

"Connie, please, listen to me. You need to make an effort to remember. You first came in here willingly. They brought you over after an incident, but it's not what they told you. It was something else. And after you came here, they convinced you to stay for a few days. You signed yourself in, said it'd be better for you, but after that, things changed. They… they did things to you, played with your mind, messed up your memories, and that is why you are here now, confused. I think you might also have some form of PTSD or something. What you went through, it was too much, so you're forgetting about it because you're not ready to deal with it. But I'm telling you, you're strong, and you can do this; you can deal with anything that happened."

He was talking so fast, in hushed whispers and looking around, as if he was scared that one of the nurses would hear what he was saying. I didn't know what to believe anymore. Everybody had a different story to tell about me.

But there was one thing I was sure about, if even just that.

"I wouldn't ever want to be here," I told him. I looked up at him, and my dark eyes seemed to have glossed over. "Why would I tell you that it was better for me to be here?"

Kai's shoulders fell. He pinched the bridge of his nose as he tried to organize his thoughts. After a moment, he tapped his finger against his nose and lifted his head.

"If you don't believe me, then just ask the director of the hospital, Dr. Theodore Faulkner. He'll definitely tell you the truth. He's not allowed to lie about this if you ask him straight up."

———

That night, I struggled to fall asleep. It was strange, since all day, I was mostly exhausted. My energy had come right after Kai told me to talk to the director. It wasn't something I wanted to think of, but it had been on my mind nonstop.

What was I going to do, go up to a nurse and demand to see the director of the entire hospital? Things like that didn't work in the real world. The nurses would probably shut me down or give me more medication to shut me up. I had seen what some of the other patients were taking and how it affected them.

In all honesty, I didn't know who to believe. What the nurse told me didn't settle well in how I believed myself to be, and what Kai told me couldn't be true because then, I was missing far more from my life than I first believed.

All I wanted were answers. Ones that were one hundred percent true. Ones that couldn't be over-thought so much that they became just another fantasy inside my head.

CHAPTER
FIVE

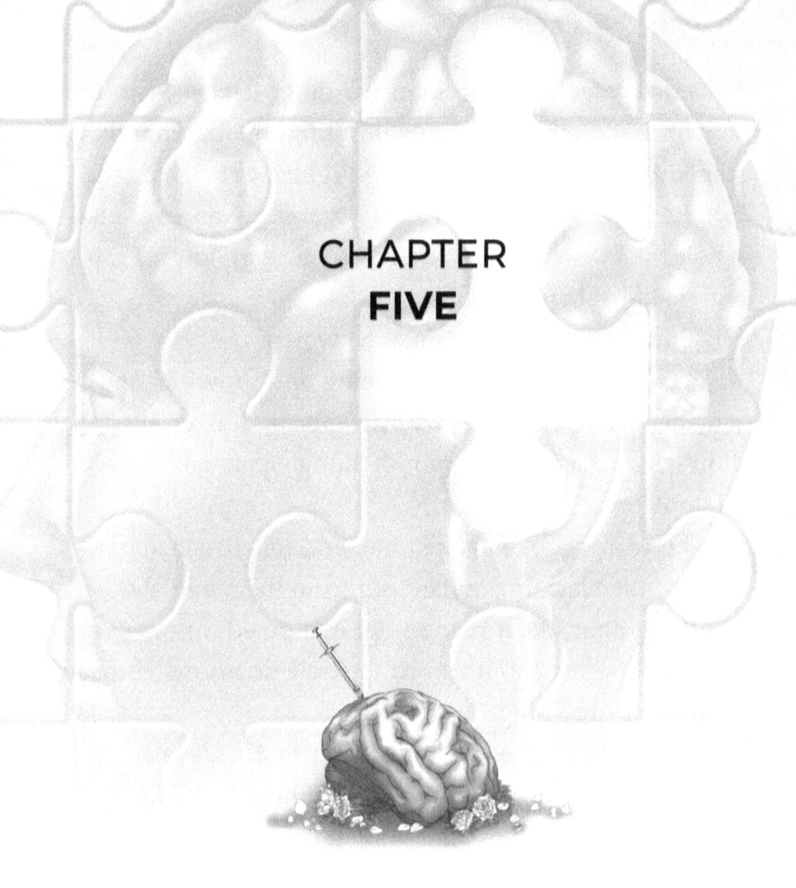

Hours after shutting my eyes, I finally fell asleep. My body was stiff as a board as I lied in bed until a dream finally pulled me under.

The darkness had made its way back into my room, into my dreams, and it was taking over the whole place. I felt like there was more than just the shadow of a crea-ture coming out of the wall, it's yellow eyes never leaving me. It was staring me down, watching me as I moved. It was a threat, or a warning. It was there to show me something, but I couldn't figure out what that something was. The twin yellow lights got brighter and brighter, and then it was gone. It had taken over the whole room, which was all coated in a yellowish tint, and inside of it: words.

"Stop!" I screamed against the words.

Each one of them kept growing and growing, and I screamed until my voice had disappeared. Even then, I didn't stop trying. My mouth hung open with every attempt.

The words broke against me, and relief rushed over me, but the black ink spilled out from them and started to fill the door like a rising tide. It climbed up my skin and reached my mouth, forcing itself down my throat until I was drowning.

I opened my eyes again, hoping that I was back in my room at home, but there was nothing but darkness surrounding me. No light. No hope. Just miles and miles of darkness.

A sharp pain tore through my stomach, and I clutched at it, trying to protect myself from whatever was happening. It didn't stop each shot of pain that went through me.

I was silently screaming in agony with my eyes wide and my fingers digging into my arms. Dark red liquid began pouring out around me. I tried to get away from it, but no matter where I went, it was there, and only spreading further.

I felt every part of my body getting heavier and let

my head drop toward the ground as I struggled to hold myself up on all fours. The sight of the words *Help Me* carved into my stomach made me sick.

My eyes rolled back, and I fell to the side. Everything went black.

I woke up from the dream with tears streaming down my face. My hope for waking up in my own bed was a hopeless cause as soon as I saw the dim light that seemed to always shine on my face. I didn't move to wipe away the tears, but instead, my hands moved to my stomach, where I traced the scars that were left there. My fingers dug into the marred flesh, and it made me cry out in pain.

My cries poured through the thin cracks of the door and traveled up the hall to the nurses' station. As soon as one of them realized what it was, they rushed to my room and forced open the door. I curled up on my side, with my knees pulled up tight against my chest, as I kept pulling at my stomach. Each line of the scar had been reopened in the dream, and I wanted to feel that pain again if it only meant I could feel something.

Two other nurses rushed in after the first nurse had called for help. They wrenched my hands away from my abdomen from where they were trying so desperately to pull the mended flesh apart. I didn't struggle against their rough hands as they held me down against the bed. I looked at each of them, trying to find the words I needed to say.

The man with the yellow eyes was there, staring at me without saying a single word. His eyes were glassy and bright, and I felt like he was trying to tell me something, but I couldn't figure out what it was. He seemed to always be there lately. Wherever I looked, he was staring back at me, trying to talk without words, trying to get something out of me.

What did he want?

I quickly shook my head as I saw a needle produced seamlessly out of nowhere.

"No," I finally croaked. "I'm not… I don't want that. Please. I just want to speak to the director… I can't remember his name, but I want to speak to him."

"Hold her down," the nurse with the needle said. "This will be quick; you need to calm down."

"No!" I screamed at the top of my lungs. "I want to speak to the director. I'll calm down if you take me to him. You can't inject me!"

I kicked and thrashed, trying to free myself from the nurses' grasp. Their fingers were digging into my flesh, hurting me, pinning me, and I couldn't stop thinking about needles in other circumstances. I had a feeling some of the things Kai had said were true, but no, it couldn't be. It couldn't be.

"Let go of me. You can't do this! You can't!"

The nurses looked amongst each other. Some silent conversations were shared, and I felt like I had a chance. I let my body relax, looking up at the nurse with the needle.

"I promise I'll behave; just, please," I pleaded. "Take me to see the director."

"Maybe you should listen to her," the man with the bright yellow eyes said.

The nurse with the needle paused her approach and looked at the others before letting out a sigh. "Get her out of bed and cleaned up. I'll talk to Dr. Faulkner. If she shows signs of trying to hurt herself again, sedate her. Don't hesitate," she stated.

I was pulled from my bed and up into a standing position. I wavered slightly as I stood there, my eyes glazed over from the dream. There was no more waiting. I needed answers.

The nurses moved me around as they changed me out of my sweat drenched clothes. I knew I was being difficult for not cooperating, but I didn't have the energy to even try.

When I was finally changed, they led me out of the room, half dragging me. I looked around the halls as they walked. I tripped over my feet a few times, and the nurses leading me down the hall cursed every time they had to catch me and set me back onto my feet.

"Can't you walk for yourself?" one of the nurses asked angrily, gripping my arm.

"I'm trying," I mumbled. "I really am."

He rolled his eyes and tugged me to a stop once they reached the office door. He grunted and looked down as I fell into his side. He pushed me into the other nurse before knocking hard on the door.

An ancient man, with the name *Dr. Faulkner* on his lab coat, opened the door and smiled at the nurse, the wrinkles around his mouth becoming more prominent.

"Please, leave her with me. I can handle this," he told them.

"She's a bit out of it," the nurse explained.

The director laughed. "I can see that," he assured them. He took me gently by the arm and pulled me away from the nurse holding me up. He looked at the two nurses again. "What? You know I'm a doctor, right? I do know how to care for my patients. Go. I'm going to talk with the patient in private."

I stared at Dr. Faulkner's hand, noticing how soft it felt. When he gently pulled me into a seat across from his and pulled his hand away, I started to look around his office.

Everything was mostly made of dark wood, and books lined the shelves around them. I wanted to get up and read them, but I knew that I was there for a reason.

But what reason?

"Ms. Fay," Dr. Faulkner said.

His gentle voice drew me back to the conversation, and I blinked at him.

"A nurse told me that you woke up from a nightmare trying to hurt yourself. Are you feeling alright?" he asked. "Are you hurt? Do you feel compelled to hurt yourself or others right now?"

I narrowed my eyes before looking down at myself, half expecting to see blood staining the front of my shirt. I ran my hand along my arm before pushing up the sleeve.

"I'm fine. I'm just a little raw from when the nurses grabbed me," I told him, showing the red rings that were wrapped around my arms.

Dr. Faulkner nodded slightly. "I will have a word with them and see what actions I need to take so that doesn't happen again," he assured me. He grabbed a notebook and a pen, and started to twirl the latter with his fingers. "Why did you wish to speak with me?"

I watched as the pen spun and then stopped, spun and then stopped, spun and then stopped, before looking up at him. If I focused hard enough, maybe I could remember what I wanted to say.

"I...," I started, but shook my head.

I tugged at my hair as I leaned forward. Why couldn't I remember? What was wrong with me? A wall was blocking me from all relevant thoughts, and there was no way of getting around it. I kept hitting against it, hoping that it would break.

"Depression usually does that," he told me calmly.

My head snapped up, and I frowned. "What?"

"Depression usually does that," he repeated. He stopped spinning his pen and used the tip of it to tap against the brain sculpture on his desk. "It makes it harder to remember things. You see, when you're suffering from depression, your brain can't process things as quickly as it should, so it can't retain a lot of the information that is given to you. It also makes it harder to concentrate and think."

"I'm not depressed," I told him.

Dr. Faulkner grabbed a file and showed me the file name. It was mine. He opened it, and then showed me the police report, which was on the first page. "You were brought here after you had an extreme episode and an overdose," he explained.

"That's not what the nurse told me," I informed

him. "He told me I threatened to kill myself and my parents…"

"Yes, well, he was instructed to do that," he told me. "You were given an experimental drug that backfired. It made the symptoms of depression worse for you, and it seemed to have wiped quite a bit of time out of your memory. During your time on the medication, it was like you were in a coma. We had to give you a feeding tube because we couldn't wake you up long enough to eat. But don't worry, we're already working out the kinks and will be making a new one soon enough."

"What do you mean, I was given an experimental drug?" I asked, my hands shaking as I rested them on top of the desk.

"Yes, we work on experimental medicine in this facility, and you knew this when you signed up for the program. Here," he said, showing me a few papers with my signature on them.

They showed that I had agreed to try on experimental procedures, and that all decisions regarding my health were now to be made by the hospital.

"That can't… I would never…"

But it was my writing. It was my signature; it wasn't forged, and I knew that much. I pushed my brain, trying to remember, trying to get the memories that were lost to come back to me.

"Oh, yes, you did. You wanted us to fix you. You wanted to forget all about those petty dramas in your head, all those toxic memories of your past, and you were more than willing for us to do anything necessary for it. You wanted to be normal, that's what you said.

You wanted the voices in your head telling you that you weren't good enough to stop. You wanted to be happy. And that's what we are working on. The trial we did on you might have been a failure, but it taught us a lot about the things we needed to improve. We have treated several patients ever since, and we are happy to say that the drug is doing much better than it did before. Less memory loss, a few issues here and there but...," Dr. Faulkner shook his hand dismissively in the air. "It's almost ready, and once it is, we will inject you once more and be done with all these unwanted and invasive memories."

I shook my head. "No... I don't want any more drugs. I want to go home," I told him. I hung my hands between my knees and leaned toward his desk. "I've got a life back there. Please."

Dr. Faulkner gave me an apologetic look and shook his head. "You can't go home just yet," he told me. "The court found you a danger to yourself and to others so they sent you here. This is supposed to be a time of healing. That's why we gave you the drug."

"You put me in a coma," I deadpanned. I squeezed my eyes shut as I fell onto the back of the chair. "I'm not a danger. I would never hurt myself."

"I have plenty of evidence here, and accounts from what happened earlier, to state otherwise," he told me. He held the folder up and offered a smile. "Take a look yourself."

I took the folder from him and started to look through it. With each page I flipped, my body began to sag more. It was like reading a story about myself, but one that was too real to be true. I kept reading over the police report on what happened that night.

I stopped moving, as all the memories of the events came back all at once. I closed my eyes and tried to grab onto each one of them.

CHAPTER SIX

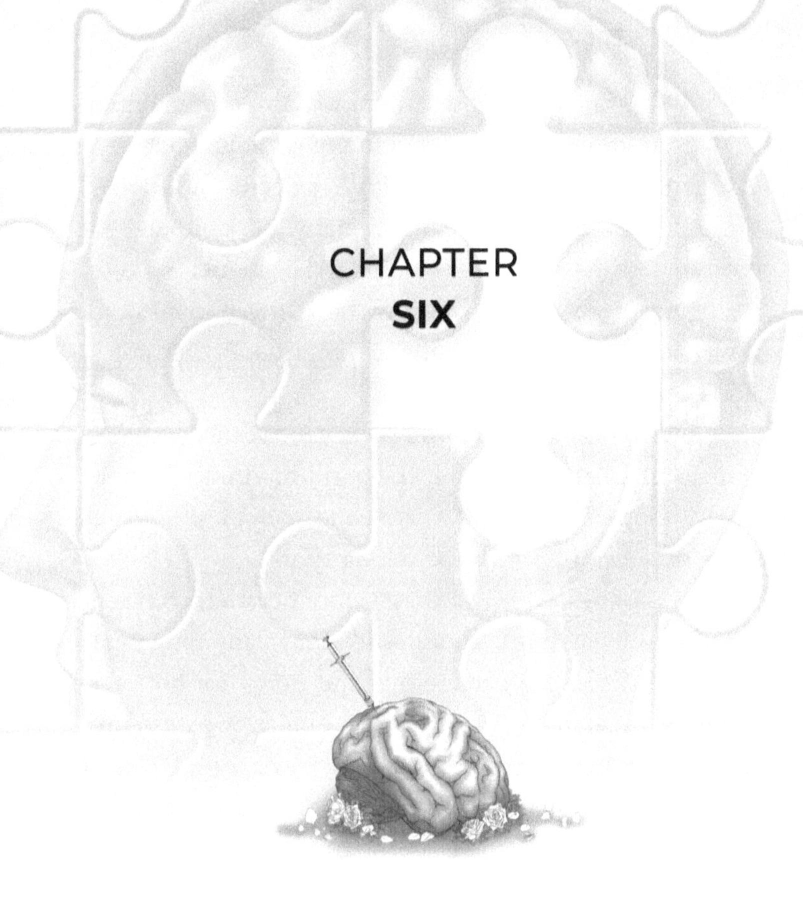

I couldn't remember the last time I had gotten a break. It felt like every day I forced myself to go through had added a brick into a bag I carried on my back. Whenever I did give myself a break, or at least when I didn't do anything, that bag sat square on my chest and pulled me deeper and deeper into a void I couldn't see.

It was a lot easier when I first started my graduate degree in physics. I was so excited that my dream school had finally accepted me. Everything seemed so new even though I had done a ton of schooling already. The professors treated me like I was an actual adult and challenged me. There were so many possibilities, so many doors that were just waiting to be opened.

I knew it was cliché, but it was my dream to become a physicist, and it was finally coming true. Everything I had ever wanted.

However, midway through my education, something shifted inside of me. It wasn't anything I could name, though. It felt like someone had picked up a piece of me and put it in the wrong spot.

The classes I found so easy before became a burden for me to even think about, and doing anything that was related to school made me shut down for hours. I would stare at a single page, draw aimlessly across my notes, or just simply give up and go to sleep.

When I wasn't doing schoolwork, I wasn't doing much else. My days consisted of going to work when I could and playing video games while forgetting to eat, or just simply not being hungry, to sleeping all day. It took all of my energy just to get up and go to class, and sometimes, I didn't even bother. Why would I? Even if I showed up, my professors would still give me zeros for the missed assignments.

The strangest part of all was that I honestly used to love going to class and doing homework. I used to love challenging myself. Then someone had to go and move that piece and change everything.

My grades started to slip, and professors who saw me as a star student stopped me after class and tried to speak with me. Even my favorite professor pulled me to the side one day.

"I noticed that you're not really producing the same quality work you did last year," he started, leaning against the table at the front of the room. He studied the bags under my eyes and how disheveled I looked. "Is everything alright?"

I simply shrugged. "Yeah," I told him. I shifted the bag on my shoulder. "Just tired, I guess."

He smiled and put a hand on my arm. "You know what it sounds like you need? A vacation. Last summer, I went on a solo trip to Peru…"

A balloon started to fill with air inside my chest, and it pressed against my lungs, making it harder to breathe. I closed my eyes, trying to focus on what he was saying, but it became more difficult with each passing second.

"And when I was at the beach, I felt so relaxed. It was the perfect getaway for me to…"

He kept talking, and I kept trying to catch his words in the air, but they felt ethereal; I just couldn't grasp them. My eyes were barely open, but unseeing. The whole room looked like a blur, and I nodded whenever he did a pause thinking, that way, it might look like I knew what he was talking about.

"Yeah," I managed to say once throughout his speech.

"So, as I said, I think you could do with a break, okay? Don't exert yourself," he finished.

Seeing it as my cue, I nodded rapidly and ran off as quickly as I could before the air completely failed me.

I managed to get as far as the nearest bathroom, where I rushed into a stall and sat down, holding my head between my hands as I breathed raggedly, tears streaking down my face. Why was I even crying? I knew he was just trying to help me, but it seemed like no one understood. They had no idea what I was going through, and I just wanted them all to stop trying to fix me when I knew they couldn't.

My boyfriend also started to notice that something was off around the same time as my professors did. He first noticed something was off when he found me still asleep on a Saturday afternoon. It wasn't like me to sleep in so late; I was usually up and moving by 6am. It'd been some time since we broke up and gotten back together, and even though things were still a little rocky, we were certainly doing better.

At first, I thought I just slept in because I had pulled an all-nighter binge watching my favorite show, but when he asked me about it later on, I just shrugged and said that I couldn't fall asleep. It kept happening more and more after that. Kyle was worried for me at first, but eventually, he started to get annoyed. I stopped contributing to the relationship, stopped putting in the effort I did before to show him that I loved him. I just didn't care about it or him anymore, I couldn't.

Nothing was worth it, not even him, so why would I even try? I was aware that there were things I was supposed to do, like doing dishes, laundry, cleaning up around our apartment, and cooking dinner. But I just couldn't be bothered. I always told myself I'd do it the day after, and instead, turned the TV on and lied on the couch, refusing to move for hours as the images I pretended to care about flashed on the screen.

He confronted me one day after he found my dirty clothes all over the bathroom floor yet again.

"Constance," he snapped, marching into the bedroom. He held up the soiled clothes before tossing them to the corner, where there was a pile of them already. "What the hell's going on with you?'

I looked up at him innocently. "What do you mean?" I asked quietly.

"I mean, what's happening? Did aliens come and replace you with some slob or something?" he asked. He looked around the room, his nose scrunched up. "You were never like this before."

I sighed and closed my eyes. "I'll take care of it later," I told him. "I've just been drowning in home-work lately. I'll do it tomorrow, okay?"

"You said the same thing yesterday, babe! Are you trying to piss me off? Are you trying to do all this on purpose so I'll break up with you?"

I gawked at him. Was I?

"No, it's not that, sorry, I just... I have a headache. I'll do it tomorrow, okay?"

I gave him the puppy eyes, hoping he'd leave me alone with the headache excuse. Did I want to break up with him? The thought had surely circled my mind. I wasn't sure he was the problem, but the fact that there was another human in the apartment with me some-times annoyed me. It was like, whenever he got home, I'd had to pretend that things were good, that I'd been busy, that I've been doing something instead of eating and watching trashy reality shows.

He'll get home, and I'd be sitting on the couch, and he'd asked me what I did all day. I'd lie and tell him I'd had classes and only just got home and wanted to chill for a few minutes before getting dinner started, but reality was, I had been in bed all day, unable to get up. I'd then find an excuse to convince him to order take-out, so that way, I wouldn't have to cook or worry about dishes.

So, yes, I had certainly thought about breaking up with him, not because I didn't love him, but because I couldn't deal with his accusing stare every time he found me watching TV or just lying in bed.

Despite the worry and the anger I was causing, none of it seemed to get through to me. I just stayed inside my head and forced everything else out. It was safer that way.

My school started to send me notifications through emails and letters on the status of my grades. Each letter had gotten more and more threatening as they were sent out. The first one asked me to speak with the graduate advisor, and then they started to tell me that my grades needed to improve or actions would be taken against me, aka, I would get kicked out of school.

Anytime I saw my school emailing me, or whenever I received a letter from them, I would either put it in the trash or toss it onto my desk, or the table, or the passenger seat of my car, and would forget about it. I had every intention of looking at the letters later, but it was as if I'd set them down in a different dimension and never thought of them again.

My change in demeanor had also caused me to get annoyed with myself. Most days, as I lied in bed, I got angry for not being able to get up and do the things that needed to be done. All the dirty clothes, books, random items I should have thrown away, were all scattered across my room and disgusted me. I wanted so desperately to clean it all up, but something was stopping me, a pull I couldn't explain.

I was filled with relief when the semester finally ended. I didn't have to worry about anything for almost a month, and once I was back in school, I would start over fresh. That was the way it had to be.

I went home for Christmas and had a great time with my family. I ventured out a bit more and let myself have a little fun. I thought things were finally turning around for me. Then I went back to my apartment on campus and found myself back in the same cycle as before. It had been a year since the disastrous return home from the previous Christmas, and the memory of it was bugging me.

When I emailed my advisor to set up my classes, I finally received the horrible news that I had been kicked out of graduate school for my poor grades. That did not help with my mood.

At first, I was outraged. How dare they do that to me? I had poured everything I had into school, and now, it was all gone. All those years of dedication and sacrifices I had been through, all for nothing. Then I felt a sudden dread that I would never be able to get my dream job, and that no other school would accept me after they learned that I had been kicked out of one already.

My thoughts began to spiral out of control, and I couldn't grasp onto anything solid to keep me grounded. Everything was a "what if," and there were no answers to give.

It all zeroed down to the fact that I was worthless. If I couldn't do something as simple as go to school, then what was the point? Why did anything I do even matter?

———

After a week of wallowing in the dark hole I'd dug myself into, I had enough. I couldn't handle another moment of the angry, self-pitying thoughts that swirled around my head, trying to battle against each other on who would be the one to do me in first.

I grabbed a bottle of Prozac from the cabinet, my boyfriend's prescription that I didn't care whether he needed, and dragged myself into the kitchen.

The cold air did little to help me cool off as I searched for a drink to wash everything down. My fingers wrapped around the neck of the strawberry vodka, and I tugged it free from the fridge before I sat at the counter. I opened it and started to chug straight from the bottle.

It didn't take long before I felt the effects of the alcohol. I had always been a lightweight, and it hit me like a ton of bricks. I looked over the counter with a heavy head and spotted a knife in the kitchen sink. Just another thing I never got around to. I grabbed it before sinking to the floor. I looked between the three things I had, the vodka, the pills, and the knife, and closed my eyes. It was what I had to do. I couldn't chicken out. I had to just do it.

In one swift motion, I popped off the top to the Prozac and tossed the remaining pills into my mouth, chasing it quickly with the vodka.

After I forced them down, I looked at the knife and spun it slowly in my hands. I wanted to send a message. That's what people did. Right?

I started to carve into my stomach, my eyes drooping to a close as I struggled to stay awake. I could feel the pull of the knife every time I started a new line for a letter, but there was no pain.

I was completely and utterly numb.

Then the knife slipped from my hand, and my head dropped forward as the pills started to do what I wanted them to. Blood pooled around me, and as my unresponsive body fell to the side, it knocked over the strawberry vodka.

I was surprised when I woke up in a hospital bed. I looked around the room and tried to sit up, but my stomach was on fire. I squeezed my eyes shut and then opened them again, hoping that I wouldn't be there, but of course, that wasn't how it worked.

What I had done was all just a blur in my memory, but the emotions behind it were still there. I was terrified of them. I wanted them gone, and I couldn't think of any way to do that besides ending my life.

I tried to sit up again, but pain shot through every part of my body, starting from my abdomen. A loud cry escaped me, and a nurse came to the door quickly.

"I need something for the pain," I told the nurse once she was close enough. I grabbed her hand and squeezed it. "Please, it's too much. I can't take it anymore."

The nurse gave me an apologetic smile. "I'm sorry," she whispered. "The doctor and the police told us not to give you anything so that you remain lucid. Let me have a look though to make sure everything is still intact." She lifted up the blanket to inspect the bandage.

I could only see a giant bandage covering my stomach, and I wondered what I had done to warrant something like that. I closed my eyes as I tried to remember, but everything went fuzzy after I grabbed the bottle of pills from the medicine cabinet.

"What happened?" I decided to ask.

The nurse gave me another smile. "You overdosed and cut your stomach," she explained. "If you wait just a little longer, the doctor will be here shortly to speak with you. He'll have more answers for you."

Not too long after the nurse left, the doctor came in. I opened my eyes and tried to sit up, but stopped myself when I remembered that I'd cut my stomach.

"I'm trying to figure out what happened. I don't remember anything."

"I'm here to answer some of your questions, Ms. Fay. If you let me. I'm Dr. Faulkner, and I'll be taking over your case."

"My case? What do you mean?"

"Well, Ms. Fay," the doctor said with a tight smile. "Your boyfriend found you after you overdosed on Prozac and cut your own stomach. We're keeping you here for a seventy-two-hour watch. After that, you may be released if we deem you stable. You will receive good care here. I have been appointed as your psychiatrist to continue your care after you go home. Of course, this is all up to you. You are an adult. You can stay here for longer if you feel like that might be better."

I leaned back and thought over the options. I had nothing waiting for me at home. School had abandoned me, and I was pretty sure Kyle did, too. I had no desire to go back to that life. But on the other hand, I didn't want to stay in a hospital. The stale air was making me nauseous, and I had never liked the white-walled buildings.

"I don't know," I said shyly.

"You don't need to decide right now, but I'll be back after the seventy-two hours are over, and we can talk about it then. You can go home to your boyfriend; he was pretty worried when he brought you in."

No, I didn't want to go back to him. I didn't want to go back to the apartment and all the memories. The pills, the vodka, the blood. The letters from the university were still scattered all over the place, and that hideous couch I had found him on with my best friend a year ago was still part of the furniture. No, I couldn't do that.

"I want to stay," I said in a small broken voice, and I saw the doctor's lips curve up into a smile that made my stomach churn.

"That's good, Constance, very good," he said as he looked at my file with gleaming eyes. "I'll send over a nurse with the papers in a few minutes so you can sign yourself in."

Little did I know then, that signing myself in would become the worst decision of my life.

At the time, I hoped that I had done the right thing by staying at the hospital. It was all so strange to me still. I was transferred to the psychiatric ward the next day, and my first day there, I sat in a sad chair in the yard, curled up in the corner, trying not to talk to anyone. Not like there were eager conversationists waiting in line for my company. I just wanted to get the days over with.

It didn't take long though for the whole lone wolf plan to shatter. Kai sat next to me, and we started talking. I could remember it now; he had been there on my very first day. But he looked different in my memories. There was something about his clothing, about the way he looked back then... But I couldn't pinpoint what it was. He'd looked different, he'd looked... normal.

Before the seventy-two hours at the mental facility were up, I began to panic. I didn't want to be there anymore. I wanted to go home and just forget about everything that I had done. I wanted to forget; I wanted to go back to being normal. I wanted to go back a few years in time, take it all back. Take it all away.

Dr. Faulkner sat me down after one of the on-call doctors had expressed his concern about me and the other patients who had to listen to my complaints.

Apparently, he was worried that I was a bad trigger for the other suicidal patients.

By that point, the meds had turned my mind into a fog. I had forgotten all about the pills, all about the university, and the cheating, and the couch, and the knife and… and… and… I had forgotten about everything that hurt. I was becoming numb again.

"I heard you want to go home," Dr. Faulkner said as he looked at me from across his desk. He shook his head before grabbing my folder. "Unfortunately, you cannot do that. Your lawyer cut you a deal with the judge, and instead of spending time in prison, you get to spend ten wonderful weeks with us."

I couldn't remember getting a lawyer or even needing one, really. The police never spoke to me. Not even once. They spoke only to the doctors, and the doctors relayed the messages to me. He had told me about the fire I had threatened to burn, but I couldn't get my mind around the concept. Thinking had become so hard.

"I… I don't understand. I thought I signed myself in," I told him after a moment. I pushed a hand through my hair. "Why can't I go home? I want to go home. I need to go back to school. I'm missing out on classes."

Two nurses came in behind me, and at Dr. Faulkner's nod, one of them injected something into my neck. They easily lifted me from the chair into a wheelchair and took me from the room, half asleep, half conscious.

The last thing I could remember was being wheeled into a laboratory setting. After that, it was all dark until

I woke up again, which I now know was almost six months later.

They had drugged me. They had injected drugs into my bloodstream, fucked everything up inside, messed with my brain, with my body, my soul. They had erased my memories and fucked up my mind even worse. I couldn't tell reality from imagination anymore. They had savaged my body, my mind, my being, my all.

CHAPTER
SEVEN

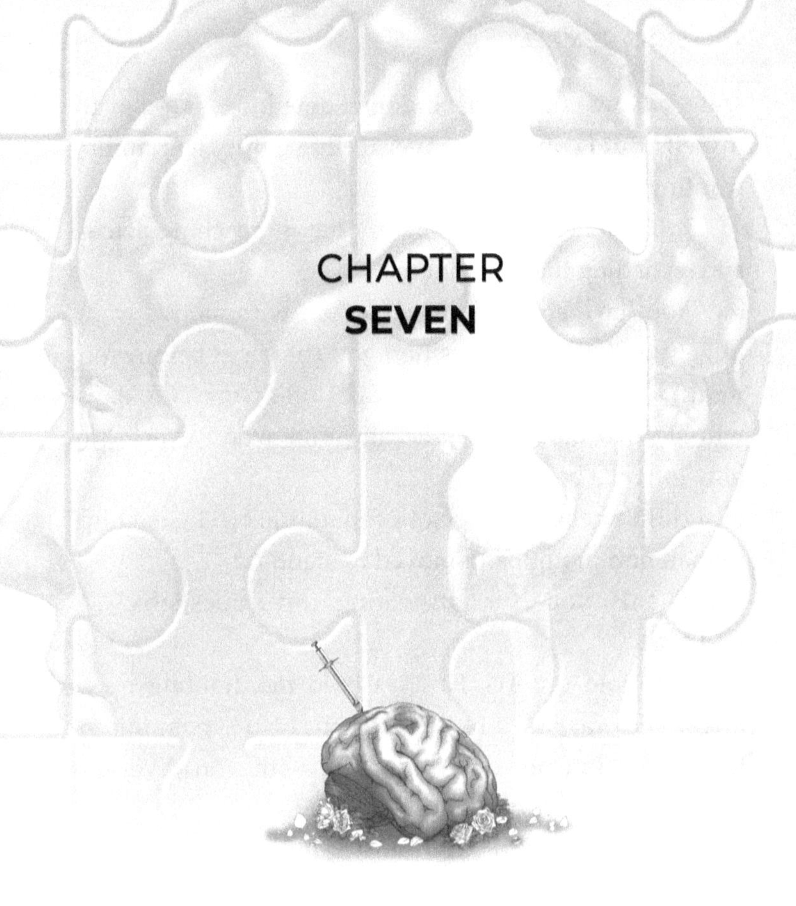

After reading all the files I had been given, I looked back up at the doctor. I couldn't believe what had happened to me. Carefully, I pressed a hand to my stomach and felt the raised skin underneath my jacket. I had really done all of that to myself.

"No, it can't be," I whispered in disbelief.

My memory had come and gone so many times in the last year, it was hard to be sure what was real and what was not anymore. I was overly confused and scared. How could I have done something like that to myself? But I could remember feeling empty and numb, wanting it all to end.

Dr. Faulkner nodded slightly before reaching across and snatching the file from me.

"You have about eight weeks left with us. We want to get you in the best position you can be in before you return back to normal society. But don't worry, the days will start to blend together, and you won't even care how long it's been."

I didn't believe that. Not even a little bit. I gave him a small nod though and moved to stand up.

"Thank you for answering my questions," I told him.

"Oh, hold on, Ms. Fay," he told me, holding up a finger. He wagged it back and forth before pointing to the chair. "I'm not done speaking with you. I've got something I need to tell you."

I frowned and glanced at the door. "I thought we already covered everything."

"No," he said, his voice becoming quite serious. "You have caused two disturbances in my hospital, and if you cause a third, I will have to take punitive action. I do not want to send another one of my patients elsewhere, especially a prison. You will be on your best behavior for the rest of your stay here, so I suggest you get yourself settled in."

"Of course, sir," I said quietly. "I'll keep that in mind."

"I do hope so," he hummed. He waved his hand, dismissing me. "You're free to go back and join the others. Your individual therapy will be starting again tomorrow at 8am. Do not be late."

I stood from the chair and gave him a small nod. I turned and left the room, my legs still a bit wobbly, but for a different reason now. More than just one threat had been made in the conversation, and none of them eased any of my worries.

As I walked back to my room, I started to think of how I was going to survive the next eight weeks. I would have to play by the rules as best as I could and adhere to the everyday schedule.

The only thing I thought would be a problem was the medication they were giving me. I had not gotten the chance to ask what they were or how they had affected me. If I wanted to survive and not get lost in the days, I would have to figure out how to stop taking the pills.

A nurse found me as I was walking to my room and walked me the rest of the way. No patients were supposed to be walking alone. I wondered briefly if all the rules were made up on the spot to give the nurses total power over the patients at any time and for any ridiculous reason.

I quickly shut that thought down. It was too close to what Kai had been hinting at in our conversations.

The nurses thought they were better than us just because they were wearing colorful rainbow scrubs, and we were wearing plain oversized white jackets.

I passed out on my bed when I arrived back to my room, and managed to fall asleep while creating a list in my head of all the things I wanted to talk to Kai about. I felt like he was onto something.

———

Dr. Faulkner watched my leave and waited a moment before standing up and gathering a few folders. As he started out of his office, he began to think about all the progress they were making in such a short amount of time. He had been working on this project for a long time; it was his life's mission, and he couldn't be prouder of how far they had gotten. He couldn't believe how lucky they were to have such willing participants for their studies.

That thought caused him to laugh out loud as he got into the elevator. A few other doctors looked at him, but as soon as they saw that it was the head of the hospital, they kept their mouths shut.

For years, they had been working on a serum that was supposed to cure all types of mental illnesses with just a single shot. It was supposed to act like a vaccine of all sorts. All patients had to do was get a shot once, and they would be set for life. The shot was meant to rewire the brain in a way that would make any kind of abnormality turn on itself and rewire back into what the standard genome believed to be normal.

The project was like a child to Dr. Faulkner, and he wanted to see it through to the end. He needed it to be finished, needed it to be done and be distributed to the whole world. He was going to make sure no one ever again suffered more than needed due to these illnesses, and he didn't care how many test subjects he needed to go through to obtain the perfect formula. His mind was his own kind of messed up. He could see no reason to stop, as he only had his goal in mind.

Dr. Faulkner's son had suffered from bipolar disorder, and it was a struggle to watch him deal with it throughout the years. They had diagnosed him early in his childhood, and Faulkner had been confident that he was the most suited person to deal with his son's illness.

His mother had fled a few years after the diagnosis, claiming that she couldn't deal with the kid's outbursts. But Faulkner stayed by his son's side, every step of the way. It hadn't been easy, but they somehow managed. Being a full-time father and a medical professional was hard, but he did his best.

His son had suffered from bullying all through middle school, and it had only gotten worse once he entered high school. No medication was good enough to keep him stable, and he usually picked fights with the wrong people. It was during one of his manic phases when he was still too young, that he'd managed to pick a fight with someone twice his size.

It wasn't the first time he had gotten in trouble because of his condition, but it was certainly the worst. One tragic night, Dr. Faulkner rushed over to see his son when he was called into the hospital by the paramedics. Unfortunately, he had been too late. There was nothing he could do to save him. He sat by his side and watched as his son's vitals flickered on the screens. He died the next morning, as Faulkner watched the numbers spike up and down, up and down, and lower, lower, until they all hit zero.

It was this death that had given him the idea that there should be a cure for all mental illnesses. It was the desperation brought by his death, and the emptiness he had felt after his son was gone, that motivated him to make a change. Faulkner had been left alone, with no wife, no child, no one but himself. And that left a void inside of him that he needed to fill with a purpose, with something worth living for.

It'd been unfair for his son to die because of the illness, so he decided to dedicate the rest of his life to finding a cure. To live for that sole reason.

He started to work on the serum as the head scientist a few months after his son died. First, he'd found bacteria that repaired damaged tissue. It'd been found in a few rare animals and insects a couple years prior, and other scientists tried to use it in their own experiments, but they didn't know how to control it, how to make it work for them. That was what he was still trying to do. Control it.

The hospital had brought in hundreds of patients every single month, some of which would be long forgotten in no time at all. People with no families, no friends, no one who would miss them, no one who checked on them. It gave them a farm of test subjects. All they had to do was treat them, sedate them, and then use them as their guinea pigs. If everything was done by the books with the patient's authorization, then no one would be able to harm them. It was all legal. Just perfect.

Two years later, Dr. Faulkner hired two new researchers after things started to pick up at the hospital, and they found that if they mixed the serum with some of the main components of most mental illness drugs on the market, they would be able to protect it and allow it to travel through the body without the immune system attacking it.

One day, barely a few weeks after admitting me to the hospital, he reached the research lab and hurried to where he knew the two lead researchers would be. As he imagined, they were both hunched over something, working diligently.

"Morning, boys," he called, patting them on the back. "I've got a few recommendations for you to take a look at. You can see who the next lab rat will be."

One of the scientists, Joseph Sterling, grinned as he turned around.

"Perfect," he said as he snagged the folders. He looked through a few of the names before looking back up at him again. "After the last person you sent, I think we'll definitely be able to make greater progress with this new version of the serum."

"Oh? And why is that?" Dr. Faulkner asked, leaning over slightly to look at what they were working on.

"With the way she reacted to the drug, it helped us figure out how it works on the brain. Also, the antibodies we put in to help ward off possible infections had ended up attacking the new tissue and the bacteria that was building the new tissue, so we know that we have to take that out," Joseph told him.

He rooted through the mess on his lab table before

pulling out the scans. He looked over at the other researcher with a smile before nodding.

I was lying on a metal table a short distance away, my brain foggy as I was barely conscious after everything that had been done to me. They'd injected me with something that clearly messed me up, and there were things I couldn't process at the moment. But I knew where I was, and I knew the three people talking in front of me.

Joseph's partner leaned forward and started to explain. "As you can see, the usual problem areas in the brain of someone who suffers from depression start to heal themselves in a matter of hours, really. I wish we could have seen the MRI for the entire time, then we'd really be able to see the growth. But then the whole thing lit up like a Christmas tree, and that's when we noticed the memory loss starting to occur. The serum had been eating at some of the healthy parts of her brain, causing a lot of damage. It doesn't seem to be stopping, so we're working on a second serum to counteract the effects. She's been half conscious ever since, and we're scared that with the amount of damage, we might need to induce a coma."

"And that helps us how, again?" Dr. Faulkner asked

"Like I said, it helps us figure out what went wrong with the serum," the researcher explained. The voice was so familiar; it tugged at something in my chest. "Now that we know we can pinpoint the problem, we recreate it without the Christmas lights… if that makes any sense."

This second researcher sounded annoyed, or maybe

angry. He didn't sound happy like the first, and it made me even more nervous and afraid.

Dr. Faulkner nodded slowly and looked around at all the other researchers working.

"Well, keep up the good work. I want the next batch of experiments done as soon as we can. I want to set up a conference call with pharmaceutical companies as soon as possible so I can get us more funding. I also want to get a patent on it so we can make some of our money back."

"Yes, sir," Joseph told him with a quick nod. He picked up the top folder and flipped through it quickly. "We're hoping to have the final serum created soon, and then we can set up a few weeks for the trial run on one of these guys. I really have high hopes for this one."

Dr. Faulkner grinned. "I'm glad you think so. It's good to have confidence," he smiled. "For now, I'll let you two get back to work. I don't want to distract you any more than I already have. If you need anything else, just let me know."

"Yes, sir," they both chorused before focusing back on their work.

Dr. Faulkner hummed softly as he walked out of the lab and onto the elevator.

Joseph turned to the other head researcher and sighed.

"He never really gives us a lot of time, does he?" he murmured.

He turned back to the microscope and looked into it.

"I mean, he *has* been working on this for almost a

decade before we took over," his partner reminded him, a smile forever plastered on his lips.

He combed his hair back and leaned against the metal table. He looked across the notes he had strewn about and shook his head. And then he glanced at me, his smile dropping an inch.

He'd been so sure that they had perfected the serum weeks ago, but only made it too dangerous for anyone to use, he'd said so himself. Whatever happened to me showed them what they had done wrong and what they needed to change to create a serum that would work. I was just a side effect, a mistake, a lab rat.

"We took it over for a reason, though," Joseph finally murmured. He pushed away from the microscope and looked at him. "He could do it, and so can we. He can't be rushing us. One wrong move, and everything could be destroyed. Any small mistake can set us back months. You know how it works. He knows that too, and still expects us to be done in weeks. Imagine if we wrote up that report and had a spelling error in it that changed the entire thing. What then? Start all over when all it needed was a simple tweak?"

The other researcher sighed. "You're preaching to the choir," he told him.

He looked at the reports again, and all the brain scans they managed to get.

The serum had started building up the appropriate receptors in my brain, and even started coating it with something that picked up on the scan. It reached about halfway before everything started to malfunction, and the serum actually started to eat away at what it had just built up, along with what was there before. I imagined I could feel the little things inside my brain, eating away.

But they were able to catch it in time, and that was when everything started to get even worse for me. The researcher wasn't proud of what had happened, but he was happy it'd happened in a controlled setting. He'd smile at me with his million-watt smile before leaving the lab for the day, and that was my last memory before everything went completely black for months.

CHAPTER
EIGHT

I went into the yard later that day to talk to Kai. Speaking with Faulkner sent shivers up my spine, and I really needed some reassurance that I was going to be fine, or at least a distraction, if nothing else. But he wasn't there. He didn't show up for any of the scheduled activities, either. It started to make me worry, but I did my best to hide it. The last thing I wanted was for anyone around me to know that I cared for anyone there, especially if they had close relations with Dr. Faulkner. It could easily be used against me.

But when another day passed, and then another, without Kai showing up, it got harder to hide my nail biting and how I was always looking at the gate of the yard whenever it opened.

"You're worried for your friend," Cady said as she stood casually next to me on the second day.

"I don't know what you're talking about."

"You do; you're not stupid like the rest. You're smart. They just messed you up. Hooked needles to your arms, didn't they? They gave you pills that fucked you up even worse. They want you to be a doll. But you're a warrior."

Her tone was soft, and she spoke while looking away into the distance, never at me. Her lips barely moved, and I wondered, for a moment, if she was really talking to me or not. Maybe she was just talking to herself. But then she said his name.

"Kai is strong, too. They fucked him up, but he's not like us. Remember that, he's not like us."

After saying those cryptic words, she walked away, leaving me alone, wondering.

———

On the third day, I was ready to give up on trying to find him when I arrived, but then I spotted him sitting in our corner at one of the chess tables. He looked like he was moving the pieces around and playing a one-sided game. The old man who usually played alone was sitting at the table next to him, also playing by himself.

My heart started pounding as I quickly made my way through the people who were already scattered around the yard. I stopped short of him though when I heard him speaking to the chair opposite him.

"I told you not to move that piece," he said with a grin. "I'll beat you in three moves tops. Just you wait."

Carefully, I took the seat across from him, but it didn't seem like he even noticed. His eyes were gleaming as they looked over the pieces on the board. They weren't his normal glazed over eyes. They looked clearer than they had ever before.

"Kai," I said quietly, trying to get his attention without scaring him.

He glanced up at me and smiled, and for a brief moment, I thought he saw me. The thought was gone though when his hand darted for a piece and moved it.

"I guess it will be just one more move then," he said aloud.

I let my shoulders drop, and I looked over the pieces before moving one on my side. I jumped at the same time Kai did. Our eyes met, and I didn't move another muscle.

Slowly he relaxed, and the old goofy smile came to his face.

"Well, good morning, Ms. Fay," he laughed quietly. "It's nice to finally see you again."

"Where have you been?" I asked, sitting back on my seat.

I motioned toward him to make a move on the board.

Kai chuckled quietly and raised an eyebrow. "I've been sick," he told me with a shrug of his shoulder. He glanced to his right, and his eyes bounced up and down like they were eyeing someone, but there was no one in his direct line of sight. He then turned back to me. "You've abandoned the chair. So kind of you."

"Don't get used to it," I told him as I looked him over. There were dark circles under his eyes and prick marks all along his arm. It even looked like there was dried up vomit stains on his shirt. "Did you not change or shower the entire time you were sick?"

He rolled his eyes as he finally moved one of his pieces. "These were the only clean set of clothes I had. I couldn't just come out here naked," he told me as he leaned back in his seat. "There was a guy here once who did that. I thought he was a nudist while everyone else thought that being naked was a part of his mental illness. I've done my fair share of reading on mental illnesses, and trust me, I didn't find the desire to be naked as a side effect of any of them."

"You've studied a lot on mental illnesses?" I asked.

I was quite impressed. I moved my piece before starting to tap against the plastic table.

"When I was younger, I wanted to be a therapist, essentially," he laughed. His eyes shifted to the right again for a brief second. "I don't know. Now that I think about it, it's stupid. I know what so many of them are like; it's ridiculous."

Suddenly, I remembered him. Or I almost did.

Smiling down at me as I lied on the metal table, half dead.

"What made you stop studying?" I asked, knowing deep down that his answer was going to be a lie.

Not because he wanted to lie to me, but because I could tell his memories had been tampered with. He didn't remember who he used to be; they had erased the guy I knew and gave me back this other version of him. The smile was still there, but he was so far gone.

"Well, I was diagnosed late in life with PTSD, and… they kicked me out of school, just a few months short of getting my masters," he told me. "I went to live with my mother, told her that I hated taking the meds, and so I stopped taking them, and then I was sent here. That's what happened to that dream."

I frowned deeply and looked away. "That's sort of what happened to me," I told him. Have they stolen my story and fed it to him? Or did they tell us all the same story? It was harder and harder to tell what was true and what was not. "That's why I ended up here. I had a mental breakdown after I found out I got kicked out for failing, and then tried to kill myself with liquor, pills, and a knife."

The piece he was holding dropped from his fingers, and he looked at me with disbelief. "You remember?" he asked. "Like, honestly, truly, remember?"

"No, I'm just pulling your leg," I said flatly. When he just blinked at me, I kicked him lightly under the table. "Of course, I remember. Dr. Faulkner told me everything."

I started to tell him about how I was only supposed

to be at the hospital for three days, and how it somehow turned into months without me knowing. Then the experiment that was done on me without my consent. I didn't mention that I thought he had been there, wearing rainbow scrubs and smiling down at me while he thought I was unconscious.

"I went through a lot of the same things," he whispered to me. He glanced around to make sure no one could hear us. "My mother dropped me off and said that I was going to stay for a month so I could get back on my schedule of taking my meds without having to deal with any other stressors, and it's been almost a year. They keep telling me that my mom doesn't want to sign me out."

"Why don't you just sign yourself out?" I asked.

"I can't," he sighed. He glanced toward the rest of the yard, his fingers drumming quickly against the table. "Since my mom signed me in here, she's the only one who can sign me out. Plus, everyone thinks I'm too sick to be able to think clearly and make rational decisions. I don't know why she wouldn't want me out of here. I'm taking my medication every day. I've been doing amazingly. I probably wouldn't even have to live with her if I didn't want to."

"Maybe she just thinks it's best for you in here," I suggested.

Kai shook his head slowly. "No, no, that can't be it," he whispered.

I sighed but nodded. He wouldn't believe me even if I told him. After all, I hadn't believed him when he told me the truth about myself. I had to wait, come up with a plan to make it all better. I needed him to remember.

"Well, let's finish this game, and then maybe we can people-watch some more," I told him. I moved one of my pieces with a grin. "I think I'll beat you in two moves."

Kai grinned. "If you were smart, you would have been able to see that you would be able to beat me in one move but now… I've got your queen."

————

From there, it became easier to be friends with Kai. Having almost everything about ourselves out in the open helped me get closer to him, and I felt more at ease when he was around. It was kind of strange for me. It's like neither of us knew the truth about ourselves, but we knew the truth about each other, and that, weirdly enough, kept us closer together.

Every day, we would find each other in the yard, and then take our morning pills before sitting down at the chessboard. It turned out that both of us were pretty good at chess. Or we both really sucked but couldn't tell.

Then we would go off to breakfast together, where I ate mostly just fruit and yogurt, but it made me feel a little better than I had before. It was also better than the sugary cereal Kai always asked for.

After breakfast, we would go back out into the yard and start all over again. We would hang out until group therapy. Group therapies were usually split by gender and category of mental illness, so there were usually a ton going on at once.

When therapy was over, we would reconvene for lunch. I liked the ice cream provided at the end of almost every meal, but we had to actually eat something in order to get the ice cream. I would eat most of my plate, which wasn't very full, and then throw away whatever I didn't eat when the nurses weren't looking. Kai wasn't a big fan of the ice cream but would still take it anyway, just so he could give it to me. He always did small things like that. Like allowing me to win at chess, even though he was better. Or finding little trinkets around the hospital that he could give me.

Some of the patients also got pills again at the end of the lunch hour, and I was one of them.

It was a cold afternoon when I was in the queue for my lunch meds, and I noticed that Cady was in line in front of me. She grabbed the plastic cup, shoved the pills in her mouth, and then downed some water. As she turned around and saw me, she lifted her tongue, showing me that the pills were still there. She pretended to cough, and I saw her tug on the sleeve of her jacket, hiding the pills now in her hand. After taking my own pills, I looked for her again in the yard.

Cady looked at me and winked as she sat on the floor next to the girl who always lined up sticks and leaves, and playing with one of the sticks, she dug a little deep hole in the grass and shoved the pills in.

I started paying more attention to her after that, and I saw her doing the same stunt lunch after lunch. She'd crush the pills against the concrete on the sidewalk and then blow the dust, throw them over the fence to the outside world when no one was looking, or hide them inside the crooks and nooks of the plants in the yard. Every time she did it and got away with it, she looked at me and winked.

———

One afternoon as Kai and I were playing chess, he nodded toward one of the newer patients.

"What do you think about him?" he asked, his eyes quickly darting over the large form of the guy. It was a new game we've started playing.

I looked over and studied him for a moment before turning back to the board. It was my turn, and I was certain he was just trying to distract me.

"I think he looks completely harmless," I told him as I picked up one of my pieces and moved it along the board.

"Hm, that's not what I asked," he told me. He wrinkled his nose at the pieces on the board and wished that he'd never asked me to play with him. "Do you think he belongs here?"

"And I answered it," I told him, crossing my arms over my chest. I looked at him again. "He's big, has lots of muscle, but looks completely harmless. You have to remember, to get stuck in here, you have to be a danger to others. He doesn't belong here."

That was my answer for most of the people we evaluated together. There was just one person who I believed should be there, and it was Frances, the man who thought he had a glass eye but didn't. They weren't sure why he thought he had a glass eye, but the doctors had to keep a bandage over it to stop him from trying to take it out.

Another one of our favorite topics was exploring all the crazy possibilities as to what the hospital was actually doing to its patients. It ranged from fairly plausible answers to whoever came up with the most creative response.

We entertained the idea for the entire day and tried to come up with who was doing what job to hold the entire operation together.

"I think he's the whole head of the operation," Kai told me as we talked about one of the nurses. He pointed to his head. "He's tiny, but he's got lots of brains."

"Okay, I need more of an explanation than that," I told him.

I looked at the nurse and listened as Kai explained his reasoning step by step.

It was a small escape from my depressive episodes, but it was still an escape. I felt a little more normal every time we spoke. I genuinely laughed, ate, and had a good time.

I was certain it had to be the medication they were giving me. No human could have that effect on people. But I did give him a small bit of credit for putting the smile on my face, even after the medicine kicked in and did a lot of the magic. He was the one keeping me sane, and I liked to think he thought of me the same way.

I'm not sure when the idea started festering in our

brains, but after watching all the patients and the nurses for a while, our game started to shift. We weren't looking over at the patients and playing anymore, suddenly, we were plotting.

We've both known for a long time that there was something wrong with the place, but we avoided talking about what we knew to each other. It was like one of those secrets that everybody knew but avoided talking about, the elephant in the room. I'm not sure what triggered it, but one day, Kai turned the game to us.

"What do you think of that one?" he asked, pointing at me.

"What are you talking about? That's not how the game goes," I complained.

"Well, it is now. What do you think? Why are you here?"

"I've already told you," I said with a huff. "I tried to burn my house down, or maybe tried to kill myself. Who knows what the hell is true anymore?"

"I do," he said softly, his smile dropping all of a sudden. He reached a hand over, touching my fingers lightly with his fingertips. "I know you, Connie, and you'd never hurt anyone. You hurt yourself because you thought that was the only way out, but it's not. And you don't belong here."

"Neither do you," I replied without thinking.

"No, I do. I wasn't taking my meds. I needed to be controlled," he said dryly.

"Kai," I said his name with as much strength as I could muster. "Do you remember when you told me a secret?" I asked. Kai nodded. "Well, I need to tell you one, too… I know who you really are."

"What are you talking about?"

"Kai… You are not a patient here. You used to work here," I stated with as much audacity as I could.

It was suddenly clear to me. I remembered Cady's words as she told me Kai didn't belong, that he wasn't one of us. She knew the truth, too; she was the reason I was so certain that this wasn't one of the lies fed to me by my messed-up brain.

Kai looked at me with his eyes wide opened, and then burst out laughing like a maniac.

"Come on, your move," he chuckled.

CHAPTER
NINE

It took me a few days to get my point across to Kai. He wouldn't believe what I was saying at the start, but as my memories became clearer, he started to remember. We worked together through figuring out what was true and what wasn't.

"So, let's go over it again," Kai said a week later. We started talking about our memories daily, trying to figure out exactly what had happened. "You're saying that I was the one who injected you with this serum?"

"Yes, I think so. I remember lying on a table, half asleep, half awake, and you were there, talking with Dr. Faulkner and another researcher. I think his name was… Joe… or Jake… something with a J."

Kai scratched the back of his neck, his eyes lost in the distance for a while.

"Joseph," he mumbled.

"What?"

"Joseph, that was his name. Is. Joseph and I used to work together!" he exclaimed the words a bit too loud and covered his mouth with a hand.

We've been trying to remember his name for so long.

We looked around the yard, scared that we had gotten one of the nurse's attention, but after pretending we were both lost in thought for a while, mumbling to ourselves, we felt safe to talk again.

"I think I remember now," Kai said. "We thought we had come up with a serum that would help, that we could use to cure all mental illnesses, but when we tried the drug on you, it backfired."

"Dr. Faulkner said that's why I lost my memories. That's how I ended up in a coma."

"Yes, and no. Faulkner wanted to wait and see if the drug would keep going on its course, but I thought it was going to kill you… We argued…" Kai looked up to the sky, blinking repeatedly as he thought about what happened.

He looked the same way I did whenever I tried to figure out what was true and what was not. "I remember seeing you there, unconscious on the table.

You'd wake up every once in a while and mumble a few words… I couldn't do that. That's not what I'd signed up for. I worked day and night with Joseph to get another serum ready, one that would reverse the effect of what we first gave you." Kai took a shaky breath in and leaned in closer as he lowered his voice. "But when we gave you that second dose, your brain seemed to almost shut down. We could see in the scan how your memory was being tampered with. We weren't sure how bad the effects of the drugs were going to be, but we had to try; it was the only way to save you."

"My memories…," I said. "I'm not sure I can trust either of them, the real ones or the made-up ones. I feel like I don't know what's real and what was a dream," I finished.

I've been struggling so much trying to figure out what was reality. I knew my therapist was right, and some of my memory loss could be linked to traumatic experiences that I didn't want to remember, but my whole life seemed like a traumatic experience now.

Kai touched a finger to the back of my hand, looking me in the eyes.

"I'm sorry," he said softly.

"I have already forgiven you."

I had. I knew Kai only wanted to do what he believed was right, and he had been my only friend since I arrived at this mental institution. His smile was the reason I was still here, the only reason I kept some level of sanity. I remembered his smile while I was on that metal table, only half conscious, the drugs messing up my brain, and I knew that was the reason I had managed to pull through. I wanted to see that smile again.

At that very moment, Kai smiled at me.

"We should get out of here," he said.

"Out of here? What do you mean?"

"I mean, out. I know what Faulkner wants. He wants to mass produce this vaccine and sell it to the whole world. And I'm not going to let him do it. He's testing people against their will! What he's doing, it's illegal, and he needs to be stopped. We need to go to the authorities; we need to do something. And we need to do it fast. I'm sure the serum should be almost ready by now; we weren't far from getting it right."

"And… your solution is breaking out of here?" I tugged at my hair and leaned closer to him.

"Yes," he flashed me a grin, and I felt my heart melting.

"We can do it; we can get out during lunch. We'll need to be fast so they don't notice we're gone. We're allowed to roam to the bathrooms freely during that time, so we can meet in the hallway, and I know my way around here. We can make it out. I know we can. I've been thinking about this for days now."

Breaking out of the hospital? It was a crazy idea, but I wanted so badly to be out, to reconnect with society. I wanted to go back to my apartment, to see the world again. I wanted to walk around the streets and be able to wear clothes that were my own. And most of all, I didn't want to die like a lab rat. It had been too close of a call, and I didn't want to test my luck again.

"Okay," I said softly.

"Really?" Kai's eyes opened up wide.

I nodded, and Kai held my hand in his, squeezing it lightly. It made all my nerves tingle with sparkles, and I wanted to let him know how much that meant to me. But I couldn't; all words were stuck in my throat.

"Three days from now, lunch time," Kai whispered to me before we went our separate ways that night.

———

I couldn't sleep that night. Of course, I couldn't.

I knew the nightmares would haunt me, and I was too scared I would wake up a nurse with my screams, and they would sedate me. I was too scared something would go wrong, and I wouldn't be allowed out the next day, or the one after.

I was paranoid and almost didn't sleep for the next three days. I'd spent the nights just lying on my metal framed bed, lying on my back, and digging my nails into my palms to keep myself awake as much as possible.

I thought about this place, and all the things Kai had told me in the past week. Kai rebelled against the hospital after what they had done to me, and seeing me in such a bad state provoked his first outburst of anger.

Turns out, he trashed one of the labs while arguing with Faulkner, and that was why he had been diagnosed with PTSD. I was sure it was just another one of the hospital's excuses to experiment on people. They wanted to silence Kai, and what better way than to drug him?

How many needles had they injected in his arms? How much had they tampered with his brain the same way they had done with mine? He'd come back full of marks and bruises on his arms after telling me the truth about myself, how I hadn't tried to burn my house down, and now, I knew why they had done it. They didn't want me to remember.

We needed out.

We needed to tell the world what was happening.

———

Lunch came around too quickly that day. We spent the morning mostly in silence, pretended to take our meds, but instead, hid them under our tongues and crushed them among the dirt outside once we were back in the yard. Cady, once more, had proved to be a silent ally somehow. We've been doing that for the past three days in an attempt to have our minds clearer, and I certainly felt different. Like my mind wasn't as foggy, as if telling what was real and what was not was somehow easier.

I even stopped seeing the man with the yellow eyes, and I wasn't sure if it was because he had been assigned to a different post, or if he'd never been there to begin with. Was he even real, or just one of the imagined creatures generated by my brain?

By lunch, my hands were trembling. I went to the dining room but headed straight out as soon as I got there. I walked around the hall, my hands trembling the whole time.

As a hand grabbed me from the wrist, I jumped in the air, and the hand covered my mouth as I screamed.

"Shush, it's just me," Kai whispered against my ear as he shoved me behind a corner. We looked to both sides of the halls, finding the space empty.

"I told you; you need to stop scaring me!" I whisper-yelled.

"I'm sorry," he said softly, his hand still wrapped against my wrist.

It felt warm and comforting, and I didn't want him to let go.

"Okay, let's walk casually, and if anybody crosses our path, you stay quiet. I'll do the talking, okay?"

I nodded, and we came out of the corner and started walking side by side. We were so close that Kai's arm was brushing against mine. Once we reached the end of that hall, we'd be at a crossroad where, if we went right, we'd end up in the wing that was destined for staff only. If we went left, we'd be back where we started. I had never gone past the staff door, but I knew Kai had, and he'd told me he'd find us a way to get through.

"Stand against the wall, and pretend to check your nails," Kai said, stifling a laugh.

I did as he told me, my heart hammering against my ribs, and sweat clinging to my clothes. He went to the door and looked at the pad on the side with all its numbers.

"Do you know the code?" I asked in a whisper while I still looked down at my nails.

"Who do you think I am? Of course, I do. I've been watching this door for days trying to figure out what the code is," he winked at me, and I covered my mouth to hide the smile spreading on my lips, and the way my heart had just jumped on my chest at his smile.

Kai punched a few numbers, and the door beeped once, twice, but didn't open. A small light flashed red, and the sweat on my forehead doubled.

"Fuck," Kai mumbled under his breath, looking to the sides again.

The hall was still empty, but we knew we wouldn't be that lucky for much longer. Kai cursed again and punched some more numbers.

The pad beeped once.

We heard steps coming closer, and then loud noises coming from the cafeteria. The steps turned the other way and began to speed up as they headed toward the noise. It seemed like someone had started a commotion in the cafeteria, and I wondered in the back of my head if Cady was real or a guardian angel looking after me. I was so sure, deep down, that it was her.

A fraction of a second had passed, the pad beeped again.

The door opened with a low buzzing sound. Kai jumped in the air, grabbed my hand, and led me down the hall, slowly closing the door behind us after we went through. We could hear voices up ahead, a few doors to the front, and Kai murmured in my ear.

"That'd be the staff room where they usually have lunch. We have to be as quiet as mice."

We tiptoed until we were close to the door, and then Kai kneeled on the floor, looking through the small gap of the closed door.

"Okay, we need to crouch so they won't see us through the glass on the door," he said. "Just make sure not to make any noise, and be as fast as you can."

Kai crawled his way across the door in a few strides, and when he signaled, I followed. I was almost giggling when I got to the other side, and we both took our shoes off, holding them in our hands as we tiptoed our way to the big exit sign at the end of the hall as fast as we could.

I knew the door led to a staff parking lot as Kai had told me, and he said it'd be easy enough to sneak through to the other side of the fence and avoid security at the gates. I had to hope he knew what he was talking about. I had no other choice.

We were close, so close to freedom, so close to the real world. We were getting out; we were going to be free.

"Are you ready?" Kai asked me as we reached the door, and he put his hand on the doorknob.

"I am." I put my hand on top of his, and together, we opened the door to the outside world.

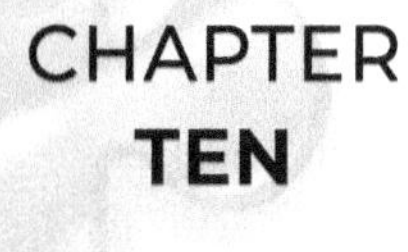

CHAPTER
TEN

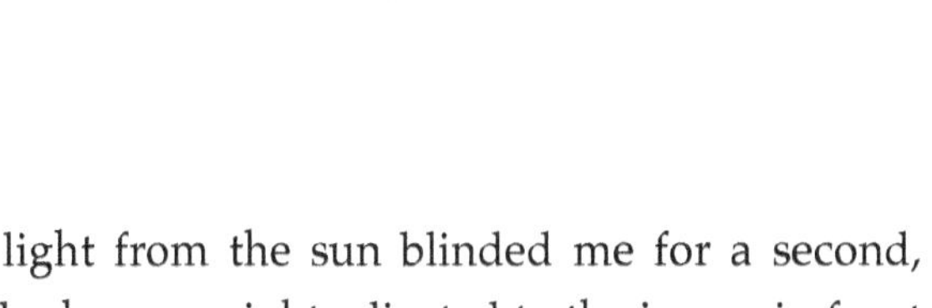

The light from the sun blinded me for a second, and when my sight adjusted to the image in front of me, my heart dropped to the floor.

"Isn't this Hastings and Fay? What in hell are you two doing here?"

There were three male nurses standing outside, cigarettes in between their fingers, and all eyes were focused on us. The largest one of them had been the one to speak. I knew him from the night of my breakdown. He'd been the one to leave the bruises on my wrists.

"No!" I yelled, moving a step back and shaking like a leaf.

Kai stood in front of me.

"Gentlemen," he said politely. "I'm Chief Investigator, Kai Hastings, and I'm taking Ms. Fay for some trials at another facility."

He sounded so confident that I even believed his words. But it wasn't enough. Everybody inside the hospital knew Kai and his story; we were sure of it. It was all just wishful thinking, believing in fairy tales, and the fact that such a silly statement could get us out. Maybe we were crazy after all, as attempting this escape was certainly nothing short of insanity.

The largest man jumped forward, grabbing Kai from the collar of his jacket and restraining him. Kai fought back, kicking and screaming, and the other two nurses rushed forward. We were defeated, ended, and the little hope I had mustered vanished as I watched the way they handled Kai, how they punched him in the gut until he was a ball on the concrete, same as I was a few feet away, hugging my knees and crying my eyes out.

"Leave him alone," I mumbled. "Just leave him, leave him."

A pair of hands lifted me up, and I felt the familiar pinch of a needle in my neck.

I saw another syringe heading toward Kai, and he was still kicking and screaming as the needle pierced the skin on his neck.

The edges of the world blurred, but I kept my gaze

on Kai. On the way back in, the two nurses lifted him up, looping his arms around their necks. They walked him in front of me, and someone guided me behind as I was barely able to walk, a hand under my elbow as I dangled like a zombie, half dragging my feet behind me.

"Dr. Faulkner won't be happy about this," one of the nurses said. "How did they get this far? It was a close call."

"Should we take them straight to his office?"

"No, I heard he was downstairs in the lab. Let's just take them there. We gave them enough sedatives for them to be compliant for at least the next hour."

They took us to an elevator. We went down. And down. The red numbers were blurry.

I heard Faulkner's voice before I finally saw him. He sounded angry, yelling commands around. I felt the cold metal underneath me. Leather straps bounding my legs and my arms. I blinked.

Dr. Faulkner and Joseph were talking. I knew it was him; I'd recognize his deep and menacing voice anywhere.

Joseph was grinning widely.

"Not only did I find the right chemical balance for the drug to work and found the thing that was holding us back, but now, I have the right patient to use it on," he laughed, and my stomach churned. No. Not again. "It's been a long time since I've seen either of them in this lab. Maybe this is meant to be."

Joseph flipped through the folder as he got closer.

"Kai," he said with a smile before setting it down.

He glanced up at him and saw the restraints on his arms. "Oh, were you being naughty?"

"Why are you doing this to me?" Kai asked, looking around the room quickly. His voice was broken, barely more than a whisper. He tugged on the restraints and cried. "Please. I just want to get out of here. Can you please help me get out? I don't want to be here anymore. You know I shouldn't be here. Help Connie… She doesn't deserve this. Haven't you done enough damage?"

"Don't worry, Kai," Joseph said with a soft smile. He pulled out the folder between us and opened it to show him what was inside. "You're going to be injected with Siero. I finally managed to get everything right. I know it will work just fine this time, and who better than you to receive the first shot? It seems fated."

Kai shook his head quickly. "No. I don't want it," he told him. He shook his head again. "I know what the vaccine is. I remember everything!"

He found my eyes across the room, and I felt the tears running down my cheeks.

Joseph sighed and motioned for the nurse and his assistant, Lorenzo, to come in.

"You are going to be connected to this scanner for the entire duration of the trial. If you are deemed healthy and sane, you will be allowed to go back to your normal life in no time. We'll keep you here for a while, of course, to monitor you, but you'll be a free man in no time, trust me."

Lorenzo wheeled in the portable scanner and stood behind Kai. As he tried to put it on, Kai thrashed about.

"Mind giving me a hand?" he asked Joseph through his teeth.

Joseph sighed and got up, holding Kai still. "If you remain calm, this will go a lot smoother," he told the man. "I know you're probably being told differently inside your head, but it's the truth. Stop resisting."

Lorenzo finally managed to get the scanner onto his head and strapped it around his chin. "We're going to run this for a few minutes, and then we're going to inject you with the serum. All you have to do is sit still."

Kai closed his eyes and rocked, shaking his head.

"How long do we have to wait?" Joseph asked.

"Five minutes to get the first scan, and then after that, we can stick him," Lorenzo explained.

After about five minutes, the nurse stuck the needle in his arm, quickly pushing the plunger. I watched as Kai jerked but then froze, his hand squeezing into a fist.

"Done," she whispered.

"Good," Joseph murmured, watching the scans. "Leave."

Kai strained his head to the side and gritted his teeth tightly.

"I don't wanna," he murmured. "I want to go home."

"You'll be able to soon, Kai," Lorenzo told him. He leaned against the table and watched Kai's head drop to the side. "How is it looking?"

Joseph grinned and showed him. "The parts of his brain that were affected are shrinking already," he told him with a laugh. He walked over to Kai and put his hand on his shoulder. "I think we've done it. Now, it's just a matter of waiting."

Lorenzo grinned and watched Kai sit motionless. He let out a sigh and pushed away from the table.

"Let's get him to the room, and we can wait for him to wake up there."

They wheeled him and the scanner out of the room.

"I'll come back for Ms. Fay in a minute," Lorenzo said as they left. "She seems almost out of it, shouldn't remember a thing in the morning with the amount of sedatives and drugs we've given her."

Dr. Faulkner couldn't hide the grin on his face as he looked over the results Joseph had brought to him. He looked at the scans, and then looked at him.

"And you are sure it will hold?" he asked.

He needed to be sure. If they had another one back-fire, then he wasn't sure what he would do.

"Yes. Absolutely," Joseph told him with a wide grin. He motioned for him to follow. "We wanted something that would scan his brain the entire time he's with us, so we connected him to monitors that watch his brain function." He stopped in front of a large window that looked into a small room, where Kai Hastings was sitting and reading a book.

"Nothing looks different," Dr. Faulkner told him. "He's just reading a book. That's not anything new to someone with PTSD. They do it all the time."

Joseph gave him a flat look before turning to the monitors that a few people were sitting at.

"These are all focusing on his brain function, and mapping out how his brain handles certain situations. He is one hundred percent cured. He's been off his meds for almost two full weeks now, and I'm certain that this is his brain if it were healthy. Nothing is there to impede it or cause any hallucinations. One hundred percent pure."

Dr. Faulkner nodded before watching as Kai just sat there and read the book he was given, and then he looked down at the results handed to him.

"This is perfect. I'm glad you got this far already. I'm going to talk with a few pharmaceutical companies today and see who wants to invest in this," he told him. He put a hand on Joseph's shoulder and squeezed. "You've done great work. Just remember that your name will go down in history."

Joseph smiled. "I sure hope so," he told him with a laugh.

Dr. Faulkner quickly walked back down the hall and to the elevator. On his way up, he studied the results again. He couldn't believe that they had finally done it. It all seemed surreal.

Once he reached his office, he sat down at his desk and logged into a video chat with seven other people. He grinned at all of them before pulling up his presentation so they all could see it.

"I know you're all wondering what miracle drug I'm trying to sell you today," he started with a grin. "Well, I'll tell you. I've had a team of scientists working on a serum that will cure all mental illnesses forever." He went on to explain all the inner workings of Siero, showing all the research they've done.

"Wait, wait," one of the men on the screen said, stopping him before he could go any further. "You're asking us for money when you don't even have a test subject who has reacted positively to this?"

"Oh, we have a test subject that's just that," he assured them. "I just received the results from the lab moments ago, so that's why they're not in the presentation." He pulled the files out and started to show them. "This patient has been in this facility for almost a year now. He suffers from PTSD and has been taking heavy medication to control it since he was diagnosed with it when he was just twenty. We took him off all of his medication, and then injected him with the new serum, and his brain has been functioning like... well, like yours and mine would." He put down the papers before leaning forward. "I'm not looking for you to believe me right now. I'm just looking for you to have a little faith. With your investment, we can get more equipment, better researchers, and we can get this serum tested out and finished within the month."

There was silence on the other end of the call as they all started thinking.

Dr. Faulkner couldn't wait for their response while continuing to stare at them.

"Call me back with your answer, and I will discuss it in further detail with you all individually, if you like. Now, if you'll excuse me, I have to get back to work. I have a hospital to run."

CHAPTER
ELEVEN

The morning after our attempted escape, I walked into the yard, and I was surprised to see that Kai wasn't there. I hadn't known him for that long, but it seemed out of character for him to not show up.

Did they do something to him?

The last thing I could remember was walking out through the emergency door and finding a group of nurses outside who'd been smoking in the parking lot. After that, I woke up in my room, not sure of what day it was or where I was. It'd taken me a while to even remember the day before, and when I asked the nurses where Kai was, they pointedly ignored me.

Time flew, and the first week without him was enough to bring all the good things I had built up down. Every day, I slipped further and further back into the dark corner I had found myself in for the past two years, and I didn't want that. Not again. With Kai gone, it felt like things were sort of duller. I had no one to talk to and no one to sit with during meals. It was odd.

I wanted normalcy again.

It got so bad that the doctors even upped my medication dosage, which made me feel more energetic, but I still didn't want to do anything. There was nothing there for me to do by myself.

Cady had come to see me during the first few days, a sad smile on her face.

"I see you didn't make it out," she had said.

I never replied, so she eventually moved away, distancing herself from me. I'd seen her through the corner of my vision a few times, lingering around, but if she had approached me again, I didn't register it.

As I was sitting with my one-on-one therapist one morning, he stared at me, and I stared at his desk. The first half of our hour meeting was silent, and he knew that I would go like that for the rest of the hour, but he couldn't have that for the sixth day in a row. It was his job to get me talking.

"Are you going to tell me what's wrong?" he asked me, tapping the end of his pen against the edge of his notebook.

"No," I told him. I looked down at my hands before I started to pick at the skin around my nails. "Nothing's wrong."

"Are you eating?" he asked. "The nurses tell me that you're not eating."

"They took my silverware away," I murmured. "Don't like eating with my hands."

"Is there a reason they took it away?"

I looked up at him with an evil look in my eye.

"I'm fairly sure it's because you think I'm going to hurt myself. I'm not going to, by the way. I don't like hurting myself. I only do it if it helps."

He shook his head. "It never helps," he told me. "It only gives you a different kind of pain to focus on. Tell me what's going on."

I glared at him before turning to face the wall on my left. On the shelf, was a small statue of a president. It looked like Theodore Roosevelt from where I was sitting. For the rest of the session, I studied the statue. I didn't look over a single detail. When the clock in the room finally chimed, I wasted no time in standing up and heading to the door.

"Ms. Fay," the therapist warned me.

"I'm not talking," I told him. "And our time is up."

I left the room, leaving the door open behind me.

———

Two weeks had passed, and there was still no sign of my friend. I still wasn't doing well. I was beginning to think that he had died. The hospital had gotten to him and killed him. It wasn't a logical thought, but it was the only one that I could come up with.

I walked into the yard after spending another silent hour with my therapist, and I went straight for the set of chairs. Most people tended to stay away from them, as they knew that was where Kai and I usually sat.

I nearly tripped over a set of feet as I shuffled toward my seat and was about to shout at whoever it was, but I stopped dead in my tracks.

"Kai Hastings," I breathed, my eyes widening.

Kai smiled up at me and waved.

"Hi," he laughed. "Long time no see."

I quickly sat next to him.

"You can sure say that again. Where have you been?" I asked.

He shook his head.

"I can't tell you that," he told me, keeping the smile plastered on his face. "But I can tell you that I feel absolutely fantastic. I'm like a new man."

"What do you mean you can't tell me? We tell each other everything, remember?" I said quietly. I tugged on his arm. "Come on, I've been so worried about you."

"I'm sorry, Constance," he told me in a soft voice. He patted my hand before pulling it away from his arm. "I can't tell you."

I frowned and narrowed my eyes at him.

"Something's wrong about you," I murmured.

He gave me a sympathetic look.

"Nothing's wrong with me," he promised.

We both fell silent. I couldn't stop thinking about what had happened to my friend. Was it the new drug that Dr. Faulkner's been working on? Had they injected Kai? I felt like I should remember something, like there was something important I was forgetting about. The vaccine had gone wrong before. What if it hurt Kai? I didn't want to think about any of that.

I looked over at him and saw that he was watching TV. I let out a sigh and shook my head.

"Well, since you're fine, I might as well tell you about the weeks I've spent without you here," I murmured. "I… well, I haven't been doing great at all. I can't sleep because of the medication they put me on, and I'm not even allowed silverware anymore. I've been sitting in this room for hours with no one to talk to. We had plans. We needed to get out, and now, it seems like… Seems like you don't care about any of that anymore. You have to understand by now that I've actually missed you," I admitted.

"I've missed you, too," he told me. He put a gentle hand on my shoulder and gave me a smile. "I just know that everything will get better soon. Don't worry. We're just fine here."

I was trying really hard not to let Kai's new way of thinking affect me, but all I could see was the stupid fake smile that was constantly plastered on his face. I wanted to wipe it off and draw the old one back on.

On our way out to the yard one day after lunch, I finally had enough. I waited until the nurses weren't paying attention and grabbed Kai by the sleeve before pulling him to the side. His eyes were wide as I tugged him around the corner and shoved him against the wall.

"Constance, please calm down," he told me. "We're going to get in trouble if they see us out here like this. Come on, let's go with the others into the yard. I want to play some chess."

I shook my head.

"Nope," I laughed. I glanced around before putting my hands on my hips and staring up at him. "You're going to answer my questions. Understand?"

His shoulders dropped, and he let out a frustrated sigh. It was the first sign of any other kind of emotion besides happiness. Though it didn't last long, and the smile was back in its place.

"Answer what questions?"

"What did they do to you? Did they do an experiment on you?' I asked quickly.

I searched his face for anything that would give the answer away, but the stupid smile was too distracting.

"I already told you that I can't answer any questions like that," he laughed. "Look, I think you just need some sleep, a little tea with dinner, and then you'll be right as rain tomorrow."

I shook my head again, my eyes never leaving him as anger brewed behind them.

"I'm not going to do that. It won't work. I'm going to keep asking you this question until you tell me the truth."

"You need to calm down," he told me. He tapped a finger against my head. "You need to clear your mind and try to think normally… like me. I'm sure you will be able to soon."

I watched him walk out to the yard, dumbfounded. Think normally… what did that even mean? That really hit the nail in the coffin, though. They had definitely done something to him.

I just hoped that it didn't hurt him like it hurt me.

———

I walked into the yard and took my seat next to Kai.

A whole month had passed, and I was sure I was going to kill Kai. Every day, he got worse and kept pushing the idea onto me that I had to be normal like him.

"You're not normal, though," I told him one day, shaking my head. "You're so far from normal, it's not even funny. I've heard the stories that you told, and that's you. The abnormal you. The real you. The guy I became friends with. This…" I motioned a hand over him before shaking my head. "This is not normal. You're too… I don't know. New. Like someone wiped your brain or something."

"That's impossible," he told me.

He turned away from the TV to look at me.

"No, it's not," I sighed. I started to pull on the loose threads at the bottom of my sleeve. "I had months of my life missing. I'm sure whatever they injected you with will do the same to me at some point."

He shook his head.

"No, it won't. I'm almost certain of it," he assured

me. "I don't know why you can't embrace this new me. I'm happy and healthy."

"You were happy before, weren't you?" I asked. I pushed my hair out of my face before letting out a frustrated groan. "I was happy before. I had a friend who could help me get through my time here."

"I'm still here," he told me.

I shook my head. "Not in the same way. I'm happy that you're… healthy, but I didn't see anything wrong with you before. On or off your medicine."

"I'm sorry you feel that way," he whispered. "But I'm still me no matter what."

"I know you are," I said quietly. I leaned over and bumped my shoulder. "I just wish I had someone to talk to about stuff. Someone to goof around with. All you do is sit here. It's not good."

My head turned toward the door when it opened, and a few nurses rolled out with a cart. I frowned and pressed further back into the metal chair.

"What's happening?" I asked.

A wide smile crossed Kai's face, and he stood up. He looked down at me and took my hand.

"You're finally going to be fixed."

"I'm not broken," I told him, jerking my hand away from him.

A few patients close to the nurses started backing away, and as soon as I saw the needles, I knew why. I shook my head quickly and started to make my way to the door, but a nurse stopped me.

"You can't go anywhere right now. It's time for you

to be fixed," the nurse told me. "Don't worry. It will only hurt a little bit."

The other patients started to panic. They tried to run around the nurses, but they were stopped and forced to sit. I saw all the people I knew thrashing around the place. Cady, the chess guy, the girl who played with leaves, even the bickering couple, were all being injected.

"Everyone will be getting the shot. There is no reason for you to resist. It will only help you," the nurse insisted before looking at me.

I shook my head quickly, my eyes squeezing shut.

"I don't want it. I don't need it. I promise. Please. I just want to go home," I cried. When I heard Kai gasp, I opened my eyes and looked at him. There was a small glimmer of something on his face, but it was gone within seconds. "Kai! Please. Don't let them do this to me. Don't let them do this!"

Another nurse came over and grabbed a hold of me. They pinned me to the ground, but I still thrashed against them.

"Please don't," I begged them.

I didn't want to forget again. I didn't want something bad to happen to me.

I just wanted to go home.

One of the nurses with a syringe came over to me and bent down my arm.

"Don't worry," she told me. "You'll be perfectly fine. Better even, so don't struggle too much, or it will hurt."

I squeezed my eyes shut as the needle slipped easily under my skin. I bit my lip hard to stop myself from crying out more. It was useless. No one was listening, anyway.

A cold feeling ran up my arm, followed by a sudden rush of heat all over my body. When I opened my eyes, I was looking up at the nurses, who were still holding me down.

Darkness started to close in around my vision, and I turned my head. The entire room blurred until I looked at Kai. I let out a small whimper before finally slipping into unconsciousness.

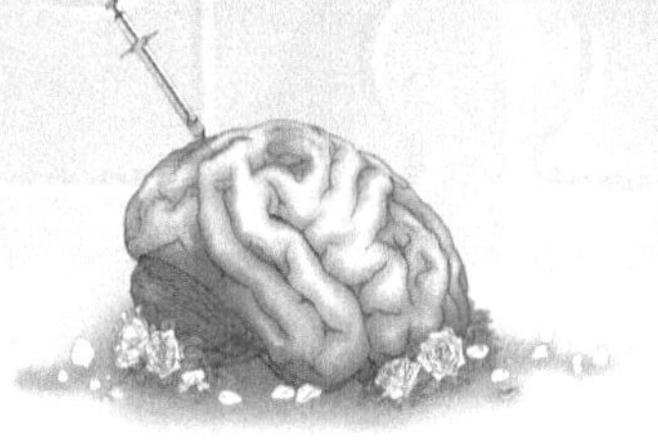

D r. Faulkner walked into a conference room full of hospital leaders and prison wardens. All important people who were eager to buy his new serum. He grinned at them as he made his way to the head of the table and set down the briefcase.

"Good afternoon, ladies and gentlemen. Thank you all for coming," he said with a smile. He motioned for them all to take a seat before he walked over to the projector. "I know you're all here waiting to hear the good news about our new serum, Siero."

"Yeah, can you honestly cure the mentally ill with… with a single shot?" one of them asked.

"Please, hold your questions until the end. I'm sure I will answer most of them with this presentation," he assured them.

He grabbed a clicker and pressed a button on it. He looked up before turning to the others, with a slightly embarrassed expression, and pressed the button again.

When the screen lit up, he grinned and stepped back.

"There we are," he grinned, earning a few chuckles from the audience. "So, as some of you have already heard at Bellevue Psychiatric Hospital, we have perfected a serum that cures all mental illnesses. We have been working on it for years, and finally, had success just two months ago with a long-term patient of ours."

He clicked the button again, and the slide changed to show a picture of Kai.

"Here is Kai Hastings. We monitored his brain function for two whole weeks and watched as the parts of his brain that were affected by his PTSD were repaired by Siero. You can see the problem areas shrinking until they completely disappeared. It's a universal drug because it travels across the entire brain, finds which neurons aren't firing correctly, and rewires them. It doesn't matter what it is. We tried it on every single patient in our hospital, and we're cleared out. Not a single person on our beds. I've got people knocking on our doors, begging for this drug. Our goal for this is to make everyone a functional human being. Someone who can go out into the world and be… normal. They don't have to worry about how many times they've flipped the lights on and off before leaving the house, or about whether they're going to have to speak to anyone. They can simply be."

When he finished his presentation, his hands flew up. He grinned and looked at Joseph before giving him a small nod. He knew they were making history.

———

I sat in my parents' kitchen as the news played on in the background. I was staying with them because, when I was sent to the hospital, I lost my job, my education, and my apartment. They agreed to help me out as long as I needed, and even helped me get a job within my field of interest.

When I left the hospital after I woke up again, the entire world felt different. It was, all of a sudden, very underwhelming. I still wasn't sure if it was a good thing or not, but my mind never let me dwell on it for too long.

My parents were happy to have me back in the house, though. My mom baked cookies for me, and my dad sat with me, and we watched some crappy movies together. Dad spent a lot of time on that couch. I remembered him sitting there from when I was a kid. He'd never liked going out much and always said it was because he was shy. But I've heard Mom use the word "socially awkward" to refer to him.

Anyway, it was almost like I was a teenager again.

Or before I got depressed.

I couldn't really remember much of what my life had been before, but if it was anything close to what I was experiencing in that moment, then maybe, I was happy before everything went downhill. I never thought it would be possible to climb back up to the top.

I didn't do much. I was never one to go out and enjoy the nightlife. I would rather stay home and drink hot cocoa while snuggled deep in the blankets of my bed. This time, when I did it though, it didn't have the undertones of absolute dread. It was something I did just to do it.

Every now and then, I would think back to Kai and the hospital, but more often Kai, and my head would start to hurt. It was a dull ache that went away almost as soon as I started thinking, but I wondered if I should mention it to my doctor.

I wanted to remember Kai, at least. He was the good part that was weaved into all the bad memories at the hospital. It was hard not to think of one when thinking about the other. I tried to talk to my parents about it and tried to ignore the headache, but every time I started to dredge up some kind of emotion, I would stop and just smile.

I sighed as I saw Dr. Faulkner's face on TV and quickly shut it off. That was a face I never wanted to see again. If I still had dreams, I would probably have nightmares about him chasing after me. But there were no more nightmares. No more dreams. Thinking about Dr. Faulkner also gave me headaches, so I always turned the TV off as soon as he showed up.

That was another thing… I didn't have dreams anymore. It felt like I rebooted every night instead of falling asleep and waking up. It was so jarring, but every time I wanted to bring it up, my mind would put up a wall between me and the words I wanted to say.

I finished my drink and put the cup in the sink before heading back up to my room. It was exactly the same as it was when I was a kid. My parents hadn't even touched it. That was why I decided I needed to change it up.

I needed something new. I cleaned out almost everything that wasn't something I wanted, and I started to move around the furniture.

But when I moved my bed, I noticed a cardboard box. I frowned, not having remembered ever putting anything under my bed. I sat on the floor next to it and started to root through it.

There wasn't much in it. Just a few hair scrunchies, an old doll, and a diary. I smiled and pulled the diary into my lap before undoing the old latch. I started to read over the passages, laughing at how childish my handwriting was. Smiling at every single page I turned.

It was mostly just things about going through middle school and the start of high school. There were entries about boys, about teachers I hated, about how I hated going to the Bahamas because my parents had forced me to go even though I was sick. It's not like I never wanted to go back. It's just that every time I thought about taking the trip, I felt sick. My father said that it was all just in my head, and I would eventually get over it.

There were also a number of dark passages. The handwriting was messy, and everything was so full of feelings. I never knew that I had gone so low in my life before. In the diary, I talked about ending my life and how nothing mattered anymore.

I squeezed my eyes shut after reading a few of the passages. It felt like something was pressing against my skull, and the pain nauseated me. I closed the diary and tossed it back into the box with the other things. I pushed the box over to the things I wanted to throw away. I glanced at it one more time before going back to rearranging my room.

———

One afternoon, I took my lunch break in the café down the street from my office building. I had been there a few times before I started working, but I preferred to sit at my desk and eat most days. But it was a nice summer day, and I wanted to have an iced coffee with lunch.

As I was sitting on the patio and sipping at my double mocha, I spotted Kai walking down the street. My eyes widened as I jumped up, nearly spilling my drink on the person sitting at the table across from me.

"Kai!" I called, waving my hand.

Kai spotted me and a smile split into his face.

"Constance," he said.

He walked over to me and motioned for me to take a seat as he took one with me.

"Aren't you going somewhere?" I asked as I sat down. "I don't want to keep you. I just wanted to say hi."

"Nonsense, I can delay my plans for you," he told me. He looked me up and down, nodding a little. "You've gained some much-needed weight. It looks good on you. You also look a lot less jaded."

I nodded my head slowly before taking a sip of my drink.

"Well, living at home, where my mother is cooking and not some random lunch attendant, helps," I admitted. I watched him with a smile, tilting my head to the side. "How have you been?"

"I've been okay," he told me. He tapped his fingers against the metal table before looking into the street. "I've been extremely happy all the time."

"Well, that's good, isn't it?" I asked.

It wasn't, and I knew it. There was an odd feeling to my happiness, like it was the only thing I was allowed to feel.

He chewed on his lip, and his knee started bouncing as he watched me.

"My mother died," he told me. "Last… last week. I think. I can't remember."

"Oh, no, that's horrible," I whispered and put a hand to my chest.

It wasn't that I was feeling sorry for him, but I knew I had to say something like that. My words held like lies.

Kai shrugged his shoulder and dropped his eyes to the table.

"I can't find myself to be sad about it," he admitted. "I can't feel anything about it, actually. Every time I do, I get this headache and, I don't know…"

"I get weird headaches, too," I told him. I rubbed my temple and closed my eyes. "In fact, I'm getting one right now. I don't know why I keep getting them, though."

Kai waved off the conversation.

"Let's catch up," he told me. "I want to know everything you've been up to."

We talked until I had to go back to work. I scribbled my number down on the receipt and pushed it into his hand. "Please, call me whenever. You're still my friend, after all, even if we don't get to see each other every day."

He nodded and tucked it away into his pocket.

"It was nice seeing you again, Ms. Fay," he said with a small tilt of his head. "Oh, and sorry. For a lot of things."

I shook my head.

"Don't worry about it. It's in the past. But it was nice to see you too, Kai," I laughed quietly. I got up and followed him out to the sidewalk. I pulled him into a hug, and I let out a sigh. "Soon. Don't be a stranger."

"I won't be," he promised as he pulled back.

He gave me a wink before he started to walk in the opposite direction.

I stood there and watched him as he walked down

the street. I stuck my hands in my pockets and was about to turn when I saw his head turn slightly.

Kai looked back at me and gave me the first genuine smile since before he disappeared for two weeks. The same smile he had given me just before we tried to sneak out of the hospital. I was about to wave, but then all of a sudden, he turned and ran straight into the moving traffic.

A car struck him at the hip, and he was thrown onto the windshield, causing it to crack. He rolled over the top of the car and fell hard onto the asphalt behind it. The limbs of his body were spread out, and blood started to pool around his head from his cracked skull.

I ran forward, pushing people out of the way as they all ran toward him. As soon as I saw his limp and motionless body, I fell to my knees. I wanted to cry, cry for the loss of my closest confidant, but nothing came out. Instead, I reached for his hand and squeezed it as tightly as I could.

My head was pounding, so hard that I had to squeeze my eyes shut. I saw images of Kai on my first day in the yard. Saw him smiling down at me when I was on that horrible metal table. His smile had been the one thing to keep me sane, to help me pull through my worst of times. He'd gone against Dr. Faulkner, for me, and ended up hospitalized for trying to help me.

I remembered our chess games and the way he used to joke and laugh all the time. I saw him sitting next to me in the yard, even reaching over to grab my hand once when he walked me down the halls to our illusion of freedom.

My eyes twitched as all the memories clouded my mind, and I tried to be sad for him. I tried to shed tears for the friend I had just lost. But there was a huge wall between that past and my present. There was a wall blocking everything in, so I let go of his hand, blood coating my fingers, and I stood up.

Turning around and pressing my temples against the pounding headache, I walked back to the office to finish my shift.

CHAPTER
THIRTEEN

I sat toward the back of the small crowd that attended Kai's funeral. I didn't want to be seen, didn't want to be spoken to. I wanted to mourn my friend's death and then go home. But I was having a hard time even with that.

It didn't make sense. Why couldn't I cry? Why couldn't I feel remorse? Did I not care enough about him? Did he honestly mean nothing to me, and I just couldn't tell?

That didn't make any sense, either. I wanted to cry. My eyes hurt with the need to cry, but nothing came out. It made everything hurt, honestly. As they lowered the casket into the ground, I stepped back and started back toward my car.

I had enough. If I stayed another moment, it would be too painful. Not in an emotional kind of way, either. It was starting to feel like I couldn't feel those anymore.

When I arrived home from the funeral, my parents bombarded me with questions.

"How are you feeling?" Mom asked.

"Fine," I answered.

"Did you meet any of his family?" Dad followed up.

"No. I left before anyone left the cemetery."

"Do you really feel alright?"

I sighed and closed my eyes.

"I'm going to bed," I told them. "I've got work early tomorrow, and I don't want to be late."

They both frowned and shared a look.

"What?" I asked, tilting my head to the side. I smiled at them before letting out a laugh. "I'm honestly fine. You don't have to worry about me."

"Honey, your friend just died," Mom whispered quietly.

Her hands were twitching by her sides, and she was visibly nervous. I wondered if she was still taking her anxiety pills like she did when I was younger.

"In front of you," Dad added. He reached out and took my hand. "We're a little worried about how you're coping with this. It's okay to be sad. Someone close to you just died."

I shook my head and gave him a hug before giving my mother one.

"I promise you that I'm fine. I'm going to get some sleep. I don't feel that bad, anyway. I'm fine. I barely knew him."

They watched me walk away before looking at each other again. They knew that something was off.

"We'll keep an eye on her," Mom whispered before pulling her husband into a hug. "We won't lose her again."

———

A few weeks later, I was sitting with my mother and father in the living room watching the news. I found no interest in what was airing but wasn't going to change it; my parents were the ones watching, anyway.

"Dr. Faulkner's new treatment for all mental illnesses is once again blowing up the news in all hospitals and pharmaceutical companies," the anchor said.

My head shot up.

"Turn it up," I told them. "I want to hear what they have to say."

I usually just ignored these kinds of stories, but maybe losing Kai had changed that.

Mom turned up the volume and gave me a worrisome look.

"Isn't that what you were given?" she asked. "Oh, what's the name of it?"

"If you stop talking, I'll be able to hear it," Dad said, snatching the remote from her hand.

He turned it up more so we could all hear what had to be said.

"The death of Cadence Croix, aged 45, adds another suicide to the count from Bellevue Psychiatric Hospital, bringing the count up to a total of four hundred and thirteen. Many believe that Siero, the serum that was injected into all the patients at the hospital, is the main cause of it. There are other suicides that have been reported, and the police say they're inspecting each and every one of them for traces of the serum.

"Notes were discovered from many of the suicide victims who carried the serum, saying something along the lines of, 'I feel nothing. Everything is too perfect.' Ms. Croix ended her life by taking a lethal dose of sleeping pills, and professionals believe she didn't suffer. The notes left behind are leaving the police baffled, but they say they are looking into all possible leads—"

I tuned the reporter out after that, and I fell back onto the couch. I felt both of my parents looking at me, and I quickly glanced at them.

"What?" I asked. "I'm fine. I'm not going… I'm not going to kill myself like them. I've tried before, and I didn't like the experience, remember?"

"Maybe you should go see a doctor, though. Just in case," Mom suggested quietly. She motioned to the television. "Over four hundred people who took the same drug that you took have committed suicide."

"I know what you're saying, but I promise that nothing will happen to me," I told her. I gave them a smile before standing up. "Everything is perfect."

I didn't hear the words I used, but my parents paled slightly. I didn't tell them that I knew the patient. I had never known Cady's last name, but I was sure it was her. It would be like her to end her life with pills, the one thing she had despised and tried to avoid at all costs. It was ironic; it was something Cady would have done.

I quickly headed up to my room. I fell onto my bed and pulled a pillow to my chest. I wasn't going to lie; I was a little afraid of what was happening. It had to be a side effect of the drug. Had to be. Everybody I had known back at the hospital was probably dead. Not that I had been close to most of them, but we've been in the same place for so long, shared so many of the same traumas.

The idea left a bitter taste on my tongue.

I turned and saw the box that I had found my diary in. Slowly, I slipped from the bed and walked over to it. The notebook was still on top of everything. I picked it up delicately and brought it back to my bed.

I curled up with it and started to read every passage again inside it. I didn't know what compelled me to do so. Maybe it was the notes that were left behind by the suicide victims saying that they didn't feel anything.

Kai didn't feel anything.

I didn't feel anything.

Why couldn't I feel anything?

I religiously read the passages over and over again like they were Scripture, and I was praying for the chance to feel like I did before.

Over the next few weeks, I struggle with trying to find the right place for myself. Nothing feels right for me. I don't feel like I'm home, even with my parents around. I don't like my job, even though it's a stepping stone to my dream job. I don't like my life.

I know it's dangerous just thinking those thoughts, but it isn't like my mind allows me to think about it all that often. I have brief snippets of different emotions that slip through the cracks of the wall inside my mind. However, they are gone before I even really have a moment to feel them.

My parents are becoming more and more unbearable with each announcement of another suicide by someone who had Siero in their system. They don't want to leave me alone for even a second. They are afraid I'm going to end my life.

I want to tell them not to worry, but I can't stop myself from thinking about it. I feel nothing. All I can do is smile, even when I want so desperately to cry or hit something or do anything besides smile. I'm getting so tired of smiling.

There is nothing I can do to help. There is nothing anyone can do at this point. I am lost. Broken. I feel like a carbon copy of what "happy" is supposed to look like.

One night, I decide I've had enough. I know I can't fight anymore, and I need to find a way to feel something again. Anything.

I tell my parents to go out and have a good night. I don't want to bother them and ruin their lives by having them babysit me all the time. I promise them that I'll be fine. Just fine.

"No, better than fine. When you come back, I'll be a whole new person. I promise," I tell them as I push them out the door on a Friday night.

Guilt hits me for a second as I watch them drive away, but it's quickly replaced by happiness. I hate feeling happy. It isn't the right kind of happiness. It's too constant.

I make my way further into the house, and then into my parents' bedroom. I find the safe in the closet, where my father keeps his gun, and punch in the code. It isn't hard. It's my mother's birthday.

"How cute," I whisper when I type it in, and the door slides open.

I grasp the handgun and pull it out of the safe. I stare down at it, turning it over in my hands until I grab one of the clips, also in the safe.

As I sit on my bed with my father's gun in one hand and my diary open before me, I start to rock back and forth. There is no other way out, no other way to live. I'm not myself anymore.

I swallow hard as I press the barrel of the gun against my forehead. Tears finally break free and start to roll down my cheeks, leaving behind shining trails.

"Please, forgive me, Mom and Dad," I whisper, keeping my eyes shut. "I want to be able to feel again…"

I allow myself to remember every painful memory, hoping the pain would course through my body and give me that sensation. I think about my nightmares, about the black ink spilling down the walls, the creepy man with the bright yellow eyes, and take it all in. I think about the night I had tried to end my life, how I had carved words into my stomach in a desperate attempt to find help. I remember the leather straps that bounded my wrists to the cold metal table, and the feeling of piercing needles breaking into my skin.

I press the cold barrel of the gun harder against my head.

Piercing pain, shooting into my arm as they injected me once. Twice. Three times. They turned me into a lab rat, they tortured me, they stole everything from me. My choices. My life.

I press my finger against the trigger.

EPILOGUE

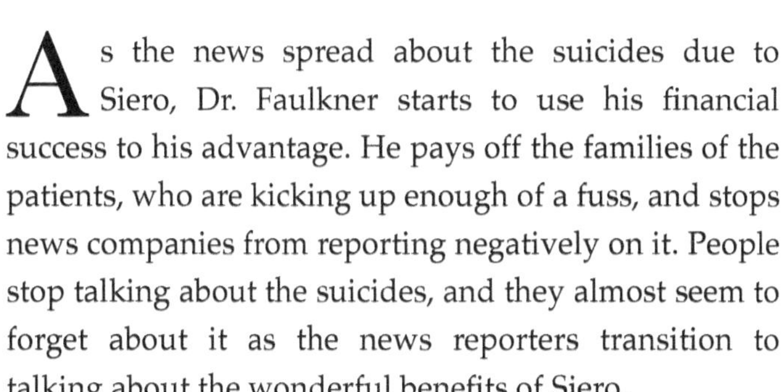

As the news spread about the suicides due to Siero, Dr. Faulkner starts to use his financial success to his advantage. He pays off the families of the patients, who are kicking up enough of a fuss, and stops news companies from reporting negatively on it. People stop talking about the suicides, and they almost seem to forget about it as the news reporters transition to talking about the wonderful benefits of Siero.

Dr. Faulkner then changes the serum to, hopefully,

lessen suicide rates, and releases it to the public. Doctors start to prescribe it to more and more people until, within a few years, it becomes a standard for babies when they are born. It becomes the new measles shot.

Dr. Faulkner's name becomes known to society; he's a savior. The man who found the cure to every mental illness known to humankind. Suicide rates drop as there are no more symptoms of depression anywhere. Crime rates descend, and Faulkner considers running for Congress.

There is a new world. And the new world is gray.

People walk the streets just smiling at each other with no real feeling behind it. They politely hold conversations about the weather before going on their separate ways. There is no more art, no more movies, no more sports, nothing that sparks anything more than a mere mild smile. People get up, have their breakfast, and go to work. They return home to perfectly fabricated families, where no games are played, where kids play alone or sometimes in groups, but are not overly aware of what's going on around them.

Time goes by, and society forgets all about the tragedy of the almost five hundred suicides committed by patients of Bellevue Psychiatric Hospital after the first doses of the vaccine were handed out to all their patients. But even if they do remember, they probably wouldn't care.

People no longer live. They only exist for the sake of existing.

PARALYZED EMOTIONS

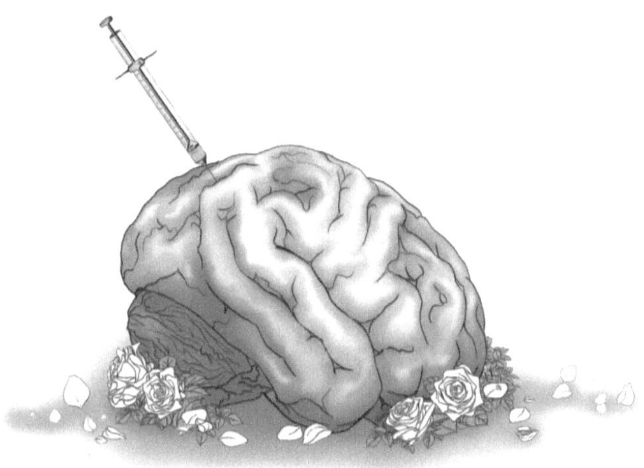

VIOLA TEMPEST